DISCARD

On Moral Fiction

ON

MORAL

FICTION

JOHN GARDNER

Basic Books, Inc., Publishers

NEW YORK

801
G174₀

A portion of this book appeared, in different form, in "Death by Art: 'Some Men Kill You with a Six-gun, Some Men with a Pen,' " in *Critical Inquiry*, vol. 3, no. 4 (1977). Copyright © 1977 by The University of Chicago. All rights reserved. Reprinted by permission of The University of Chicago Press.

Library of Congress Cataloging in Publication Data

Gardner, John Champlin, 1933–
   On moral fiction.

   Includes bibliographical references.
   1. Literature and morals.   2. Arts and morals.
I. Title.
PN49.G345   801   77-20409
ISBN: 0-465-05225-8

Copyright © 1978 by John Gardner
Printed in the United States of America
DESIGNED BY VINCENT TORRE
10 9 8 7 6 5 4

For Liz

810590

ACKNOWLEDGMENTS

Some of the writing in this book has appeared, in different form, in *Critical Inquiry, The Hudson Review,* and *The Western Humanities Review,* and some of the ideas here I've borrowed, usually in modified form, from friends, not only from those with whom I usually agree, like Edmund Epstein, but also from those with whom I usually disagree, like William Gass.

PART I

PREMISES ON ART AND MORALITY

1

BOOK as wide-ranging as this one needs a governing metaphor to give it at least an illusion that all is well:

It was said in the old days that every year Thor made a circle around Middle-earth, beating back the enemies of order. Thor got older every year, and the circle occupied by gods and men grew smaller. The wisdom god, Woden, went out to the king of the trolls, got him in an armlock, and demanded to know of him how order might triumph over chaos.

"Give me your left eye," said the king of the trolls, "and I'll tell you."

Without hesitation, Woden gave up his left eye. "Now tell me."

The troll said, "The secret is, *Watch with both eyes!*"

Woden's left eye was the last sure hope of gods and men in their kingdom of light surrounded on all sides by darkness. All we have left is Thor's hammer, which represents not brute force but art, or, counting both hammerheads, art and criticism. Thor is no help. Like other gods, he has withdrawn from our immediate view. We have only his weapon, abandoned beside a fencepost in high weeds, if we can figure out how to use it. This book is an attempt to develop a set of instructions, an analysis of what has gone wrong in recent years with the various arts—especially fiction, since that is the art on which I'm best informed—and what has gone wrong with criticism.

The language of critics, and of artists of the kind who pay attention to critics, has become exceedingly odd: not talk about feelings or intellectual affirmations—not talk about moving and surprising twists of plot or wonderful characters and ideas—but sentences full of large words like *hermaneutic, heuristic, structuralism, formalism,* or *opaque language,* and full of fine distinctions—for instance those between *modernist* and *post-modernist*—that would make even an intelligent cow suspicious. Though more difficult than ever before to read, criticism has become trivial.

The trivial has its place, its entertainment value. I can think of no good reason that some people should not specialize in the behavior of the left-side hairs on an elephant's trunk. Even at its best, its most deadly serious, criticism, like art, is partly a game, as all good critics know. My objection is not to the game but to the fact that contemporary critics have for the most part lost track of the point of their game, just as artists, by and large, have lost track of the point of theirs. Fiddling with the hairs on an elephant's nose is indecent when the elephant happens to be standing on the baby.

At least in America art is not thought capable, these days, of tromping on babies. Yet it does so all the time, and what is worse, it does so with a bland smile. I've watched writers, composers, and painters knocking off their "works" with their left hands. Nice people, most of them. Artists are generally pleasant people, childlike both in love and hate, intending no harm when they turn out bad paintings, compositions, or books. Indeed, their ambition guarantees that they will do the best they know how to do or think they ought to do. The error is less in their objects than in their objectives. "Art is play, or partly play," they'll tell you with an engaging smile, serving up their non-nutritious fare with the murderous indifference of a fat girl serving up hamburgers. What they say is true enough, as far as it goes, and nothing is more tiresome than the man who keeps hollering, "Hey, let's be *serious!*" but that is what we must holler.

In a world where nearly everything that passes for art is tinny and commercial and often, in addition, hollow and academic, I argue—by reason and by banging the table—for an old-fashioned view of what art is and does and what the fundamental business of critics ought therefore to be. Not that I want joy taken out of the arts; but even frothy entertainment is not harmed by a touch of moral responsibility, at least an evasion of too fashionable simplifications. My basic message throughout this book is as old as the hills, drawn from Homer, Plato, Aristotle, Dante, and the rest, and standard in Western civilization down through the eighteenth century; one would think all critics and artists should be thoroughly familiar with it, and perhaps many are. But my experience is that in university lecture halls, or in kitchens at midnight, after parties, the traditional view of art strikes most people as strange news.

The traditional view is that true art is moral: it seeks to improve life, not debase it. It seeks to hold off, at least for a while, the twilight of the gods and us. I do not deny that art, like criticism, may legitimately celebrate the trifling. It may joke, or mock, or while away the time. But trivial art has no meaning or value except

5

in the shadow of more serious art, the kind of art that beats back the monsters and, if you will, makes the world safe for triviality. That art which tends toward destruction, the art of nihilists, cynics, and merdistes, is not properly art at all. Art is essentially serious and beneficial, a game played against chaos and death, against entropy. It is a tragic game, for those who have the wit to take it seriously, because our side must lose; a comic game—or so a troll might say—because only a clown with sawdust brains would take our side and eagerly join in.

Like legitimate art, legitimate criticism is a tragicomic holding action against entropy. Life is all conjunctions, one damn thing after another, cows *and* wars *and* chewing gum *and* mountains; art—the best, most important art—is all subordination: guilt *because of* sin *because of* pain. (All the arts treat subordination; literature is merely the most explicit about what leads to what.) Art builds temporary walls against life's leveling force, the ruin of what is splendidly unnatural in us, consciousness, the state in which not all atoms are equal. In corpses, entropy has won; the brain and the toenails have equal say. Art asserts and reasserts those values which hold off dissolution, struggling to keep the mind intact and preserve the city, the mind's safe preserve. Art rediscovers, generation by generation, what is necessary to humanness. Criticism restates and clarifies, reenforces the wall. Neither the artist nor the critic believes, when he stands back from his work, that he will hold off the death of consciousness forever; and to the extent that each laughs at his feeble construction he knows that he's involved in a game. As long as he keeps the whole picture in mind—the virtues and hairline cracks in the wall, the enormous power of the turbulence outside—the artist and after him the critic can do what he does with reasonable efficiency. The moment the artistic or critical mind loses sight of the whole, focusing all attention on, say, the flexibility of the trowel, the project begins to fail, the wall begins to crack with undue rapidity (we expected all along that the wall would crack, but not like this! not there and there too and even there!) and the builder becomes panicky, ferocious, increasingly inefficient.

No one is more cranky, more irascible, more quick to pontificate on the virtues of his effort than the artist who knows, however dimly, that he's gotten off the track, that his work has nothing to do with what Shakespeare did, or Brahms, or Rembrandt. Having gotten into art for love of it, and finding himself unable to support, in his own art, what true art has supported since time began, he turns defensively on everything around him. He becomes rabid, often rabidly cynical, insisting on the importance of his trivia. He sends to his fellow artists sharply worded notes: "Literature is exhausted", "Painting has no base of reference but itself." Critics do the same, some of them lashing out at real or imagined enemies, others focusing increasing intellectual energy on trifles. Some labor to determine, for instance, exactly what the term *post-modern* ought to mean, distracted from the possiblity that it ought to mean nothing, or nothing significant, that the critic's interest in the idea rises from a mistaken assumption comparable to the assumption which led to the medieval category "Animals Which Exist in Fire." In this case, the notion is that art is progressive, like science, so that Hemingway somehow leads logically to Bellow, and Bellow to Barthelme, the same notion that makes Turner an important painter when he's viewed as an early impressionist, a minor one when he's viewed as the last neoclassicist. When the critical game turns humorless in this way, taking dire positions and defending them with force, the critic's mistakes become serious matters. In art as in politics, well-meant, noble-sounding errors can devalue the world.

Part of the problem is that, even at its best, criticism—including the criticism set down by poets and novelists, composers, painters, sculptors, dancers, and photographers—is easier than authentic art to grasp and treat as immutable doctrine. Depending as it does on logic and scheme, on arguments well argued, criticism uses parts of the mind more readily available to us than are the faculties required for art. And since the tests of criticism are completeness and coherence, whereas art's validity can only be tested by an imaginative act on the reader's part, criticism is easier to read; that is, it does not require the involvement of as many faculties of the mind.

The critic' proper business is explanation and evaluation, which means he must make use of his analytic powers to translate the concrete to the abstract. He knows art loses in the translation but also gains: people who couldn't respond to the work can now go back to it with some idea of what to look for, and even if all they see is what the critic has told them to see, at least they've seen something. To understand a critic, one needs a clear head and a sensitive heart, but not great powers of imagination. To understand a complex work of art, one must be something of an artist oneself. Thus criticism and art, like theology and religion, are basically companions but not always friends. At times they may be enemies.

By its nature, criticism makes art sound more intellectual than it is—more calculated and systematic. Analytic intelligence is not intelligence of the kind that leads us through imitated concrete experience to profound intellectual and emotional understanding, but a cooler, more abstract kind that isolates complicated patterns and notes the subtleties or wider implications of what the artist has said. The best critical intelligence, capable of making connections the artist himself may be blind to, is a noble thing in its place; but applied to the making of art, cool intellect is likely to produce superficial work, either art which is all sensation or art which is all thought. We see this wherever we find art too obviously constructed to fit a theory, as in the music of John Cage or in the recent fiction of William Gass. The elaboration of texture for its own sake is as much an intellectual, even academic exercise as is the reduction of plot to pure argument or of fictional characters and relationships to bloodless embodiments of ideas. True art is a conduit between body and soul, between feeling unabstracted and abstraction unfelt.

Philosophy is more concerned with coherence than with what William James called life's "buzzing, blooming confusion." And what philosophy does for actuality, critics do for art. Art gropes. It stalks like a hunter lost in the woods, listening to itself and to everything around it, unsure of itself, waiting to pounce. This is not to deny that art and philosophy are related. When a metaphysical system breaks down, or seems to have broken down, the forms of art which supported that system no longer feel true or adequate. Thus Hart Crane, when he found the sky "ungoded," fractured poetry, and thus Crane's friend Jean Toomer, when old forms betrayed his mystical, kaleidoscopic intuition—a religious intuition, quite the opposite of Crane's—abandoned traditional forms of fiction. But neither smashing of tradition was philosophical. Crane and Toomer were hunting, not stating. When modes of art change, the change need not imply philosophical progress; it usually means only that the hunter has exhausted one part of the woods and has moved to a new part, or to a part exhausted earlier, to which the prey may have doubled back. Art is not philosophy but, as

R. G. Collingwood said, "the cutting edge of philosophy."

To put all this in the form of another traditional metaphor, aesthetic styles—patterns for communicating feeling and thought—become dull with use, like carving knives, and since dullness is the chief enemy of art, each generation of artists must find new ways of slicing the fat off reality. Sometimes this happens as artists trace into strange new territory the implications in the work of some genius, as Brahms, Debussey, Wagner, and the rest followed out suggestions in Beethoven, or as Dos Passos, Hemingway, Faulkner, and others developed ideas of James Joyce and Gertrude Stein. Sometimes the new comes in reaction against the old. Thus the social realism of O'Hara's day gives way to the vogue of "fabulism," and fabulism will no doubt in turn give way to surrealism, or realism, or something else. Some critics hail the change as insightful, the expression of a new apprehension of reality. The decline of the closely plotted novel or the structured play, for instance, or the abnegation of melody in music, or of the identifiable image in photography and cinematography, is hailed as an appropriate artistic reflection of our discovery that the universe is not orderly. But this is, as I've said, misleading.

It's misleading for two main reasons. One is that its assertion about reality is naive. Despite the aha's of some modern philosophers, metaphysical systems do not, generally speaking, break down, shattered by later, keener insight; they are simply abandoned— sometimes after endless tinkering and clumsy renovation—like drafty old castles. This is of course part of Kafka's joke in *The Castle* and elsewhere; and Kafka is often cited as one of the artists who "show us" the failure of traditional thought, how the castle of metaphysics has proved a ghastly mistake though expanded, patched, and toggled, century on century, by people working in increasing desperation and despair. But Kafka's art is more subtle, more comic and ironic, than such a reading admits. Much of the power of Kafka's work comes from our sense as we read that real secrets have been forgotten, real clues are being missed, a wholeness of vision that was once adequate has been lost and is now tragicomically unrecoverable. Melville says much the same in *The Confidence Man* and, though his tone is in this case very different, at the end of *Israel Potter*. The Yankee Christian virtues Israel Potter represents have not been disqualified or proved inadequate; they have simply lost currency, which is to say they are no longer clearly understood and have fallen out of style.

With their intuitive philosophies, thinkers like Nietzsche and Kierkegaard overwhelmed such schools as the Oxford idealists, though nowhere in all their writings do they refute or for that matter show that they clearly understand the idealist position on even so basic a matter as whether or not there can be rational goodness. Thus the tradition which runs from Bradley and Collingwood to George Sidgewick and Brand Blanchard, not to mention contemporary phenomenologists, is not in fact outmoded but merely unpopular—*believed* to be outmoded, like sonata form or the novel with fully shaped characters and plot—and the victorious positions of existentialists, absurdists, positivists, and the rest are not demonstrably more valid but only, for the moment, more hip. There are already signs that the moment of these, too, is over. The truth is certainly that the universe is partly structured, partly unstructured; otherwise entropy would be total, there would be no one to resist. (This has now been proved mathematically. It was, you recall, the problem Einstein worked at on his deathbed.) As long as philosophers focus on parts of the universe that are unstructured, and argue by analogy that good and evil, even love of one's children, may be equally inchoate, and as long as most people continue to believe them, the playwright or novelist, sculptor or composer, who reflects such notions in his work may seem "adequate" or "interesting." The moment philosophers and the direct or indirect suivants of philosophers shift their main focus to the part of the universe that is patently structured, and make achieved order the basis of their analogies, the artistic fascination with universal chaos and death begins to sound inadequate and boring.

The too-close identification of stylistic innovation and philosophical insight is misleading for another, more important reason: it tends toward misapprehension of the artistic process and, insofar as the misapprehension persuades, encourages the artist to work in the wrong way, at the same time encouraging the rest of humanity to praise him for his sin.

The philosophical implications of style are at least partly accidental, not essential; that is, not initially purposeful, pre-planned, or at any rate not entirely so. Art's process values chance. Good writers invent style at least partly in order to be interesting to themselves and others—they mysteriously "find" it as they "find" their plots or subjects—and only then, as the style is emerging, do they try to work out the philosophical implications of the creature they've stumbled onto. Original style arises out of personality and the freak accident of the artist's particular aesthetic experience—the fortuitous combination, during a writer's childhood of (let us say) Tolstoy, Roy Rogers, and the chimpanzee act at the St. Louis Zoo. Only after the style has begun to assert itself does the writer's intellect make sense of it, discover or impose some purpose and develop the style further, this time in full consciousness of what it portends. It's as if a scientist were to assert once again the existence of flogiston, with the aim of gaining the world's attention and giving occupation to his quick, cranky mind, and then were to elaborate a complete metaphysical system in support of his assertion. That would generally be bad science; but art is something else. Good science normally makes hypotheses based on observation or probability; art deals, at its best, with what has never been observed, or observed only peripherally—darts from what is to what might have been—asking with total interest and sobriety such questions as "What if apple trees could talk?" or "What if the haughty old woman next door should fall in love with Mr. Powers, our mailman?" The artist's imagination, or the world it builds, is the laboratory of the unexperienced, both the heroic and the unspeakable.

Art is as original and important as it is precisely because it does *not* start out with clear knowledge of what it means to say. Out of the artist's imagination, as out of nature's inexhaustible well, pours one thing after another. The artist composes, writes, or paints just as he dreams, seizing whatever swims close to his net. This, not the world seen directly, is his raw material. This shimmering mess of loves and hates—fishing trips taken long ago with Uncle Ralph, a 1940 green Chevrolet, a war, a vague sense of what makes a novel, a symphony, a photograph—this is the clay the artist must shape into an object worthy of our attention; that is, our tears, our laughter, our thought. As students of aesthetics used to say, art combines fancy and judgment. Or as Schiller once put it in a letter to a friend, what happens in the case of the creative mind is that "the intellect has withdrawn its watchers from the gates, and the ideas rush in pell-mell, and only then does [the creative mind] review and inspect the multitude." As a general rule, the artist who begins with a doctrine to promulgate, instead of a rabble multitude of ideas and emotions, is beaten before he starts. True art imitates nature's total process: endless blind experiment (fish that climb trees, hands with nine fingers, shifts in and out of tonality) and then ruthless selectivity—the artist's sober judgments, like a lion's, of what can be killed, what is better left alone, such as (for the lion) rhinos and certain nasty snakes. Art, in sworn opposition to chaos, discovers *by its process* what it can say. That is art's morality. Its full meaning is beyond paraphrase, though critical paraphrase may make difficult things easier, even to the artist himself. Hence the old but important commonplace: the meaning of a work of art is the work of art. This is of course not quite to say, as John Barth does in *Chimera,* "The key to the treasure is the treasure," since that implies (at least on one level) that having the key we should treasure the key and look for nothing more. What art opens up for us is "the real," a treasure vastly beyond the value of the key; but neither reality nor art's imitation is expressible in the language of abstract thought.

Criticism, when most interesting and vital, tends toward art, that is, bad science, making up fictions about fictions. To make the concrete abstract is inescapably to distort. It turns emotional development into logical progression, artistic vision into thesis. The trouble is that whereas the artist's fiction is complex beyond our capacity to express it, the critic's fictions—art cleaned up and clarified, at worst reduced to what the critic considers its main point—can easily take on the authority of Right. The words of a confident, earnest critic can lock up museums, keep books from publication, and enhance the sale of things unworthy. I need not give many examples. Despite Hindemith's discovery that "undertones" govern the tonality of a musical cluster and despite Schonberg's own disavowal of the atonal method, the popular critical pseudodoxy that atonality musically imitates Einsteinian relativity has for years promoted a music which—in absolute form and without Schonberg's passion or genius—is in fact gibberish, a music which ignores or violates the structure of the mind: we literally cannot hear it. Or take literature. For years the Oz books were kept away from children because pseudo-critics (second-rate educators and amateur psychiatrists) decided that beheadings, however comic or acceptable in context, meant castration. On the other hand, mountains of unspeakable books, paintings, symphonies, and so on, have been dumped on long-suffering humanity in recent years because mediocre critics have wrongly claimed for them astute perceptions on the problems of, for instance, blacks and women. One might suppose such a vogue would at least help true art on the same subjects; but not so. A really good book or painting concerning blacks or women is as hard to sell now as it ever was. True art is too complex to reflect the party line. Art that tries hard to tell the truth unretouched is difficult and often offensive. It tears down our heroes and heart-warming convictions, violates canons of politeness and humane compromise.

I have claimed that art is essentially and primarily moral—that is, life-giving—moral in its process of creation and moral in what it says. If people all over Europe killed themselves after reading Goethe's *Sorrows of Young Werther,* then either Goethe's book was false art or his readers misunderstood. Only in lament does the artist cry out, "Birds build but not I build," and the lament points to how things ought to be: art builds; it never stands pat; it destroys only evil. If art destroys good, mistaking it for evil, then that art is false, an error; it requires denunciation. This, I have

15

claimed, is what true art is about—preservation of the world of gods and men. True criticism praises true art for what it does—praises as plainly and comprehensively as possible—and denounces false art for its failure to do art's proper work. No easy task, the task of the critic, since the trolls are masters of disguise.

Most art these days is either trivial or false. There has always been bad art, but only when a culture's general world view and aesthetic theory have gone awry is bad art what most artists strive for, mistaking bad for good. In Plato's Athens or Shakespeare's London, who would have clapped for the merdistes? For the most part our artists do not struggle—as artists have traditionally struggled—toward a vision of how things ought to be or what has gone wrong; they do not provide us with the flicker of lightning that shows us where we are. Either they pointlessly waste our time, saying and doing nothing, or they celebrate ugliness and futility, scoffing at good. Every new novelist, composer, and painter— or so we're told—is more "disturbing" than the last. The good of humanity is left in the hands of politicians.

Contemporary criticism is not much better. In all the arts, our criticism is for the most part inhumane. We are rich in schools which speak of how art "works" and avoid the whole subject of what work it ought to do. Armies of musicologists tell us by vector analysis, aided by computers, that a notable feature of Brahms' style is his tendency to move downward by thirds and that Beethoven is motive-obsessive. Such analysis can be equally insightful on the work of the common bluejay; it has nothing to say on which is better, Brahms or the bluejay. As for poetry and fiction, since the days of the New Critics (not all of them were bad) we've been hearing about technique, how part must fit with part, no matter to what purpose. Not only can such an approach tell us nothing about great works of art that are clumsily put together, like *Paradise Lost* or *Piers Plowman*, to say nothing of *The Brothers Karamazov* or *War and Peace*, it cannot even show us the difference between a well-made vital work like John Fowles' *Daniel Martin*, and an empty but well-made husk like John Barth's *Giles Goat-boy*. Structuralists, formalists, linguistic philosophers who tell us that works of art are like trees—simply objects for perception—all avoid on principle the humanistic questions: who will this work of art help? what baby is it squashing? The business of criticism has become definition, morality reduced to the positivist ideal of clarity. The trouble is that clarity on the wrong subject can be dangerously misleading, as when we define Count Fosco's crocodile as a smiling animal weighing four hundred pounds.

2

NOTHING could be more obvious, it seems to me, than that art should be moral and that the first business of criticism, at least some of the time, should be to judge works of literature (or painting or even music) on grounds of the production's moral worth. By "moral" I do not mean some such timid evasion as "not too blatantly *im*moral." It is not enough to say, with the support of mountains of documentation from sociologists, psychiatrists, and the New York City Police Department, that television is a bad influence when it actively encourages pouring gasoline on people and setting fire to them. On the contrary, televison—or any other more or less artistic medium—is good (as opposed to pernicious or vacuous) only when it has a clear positive moral effect, presenting valid models for imitation, eternal verities worth keeping in mind, and a benevolent vision of the possible which can inspire and incite human beings toward virtue, toward life affirmation as opposed to destruction or indifference. This obviously does not mean that art should hold up cheap or cornball models of behavior, though even those do more good in the short run than does, say, an attractive bad model like the quick-witted cynic so endlessly celebrated in light-hearted films about voluptuous women and international intrigue. In the long run, of course, cornball morality leads to rebellion and the loss of faith. I do not mean, either, that what the world needs is didactic art. Didacticism and true art are immiscible; and in any case, nothing guarantees that didacticism will be moral. Think of *Mein Kampf*. True art is *by its nature* moral. We recognize true art by its careful, thoroughly honest search for and analysis of values. It is not didactic because, instead of teaching by authority and force, it explores, open-mindedly, to learn what it should teach. It clarifies, like an experiment in a chemistry lab, and confirms. As a chemist's experiment tests the laws of nature and dramatically reveals the truth or falsity of scientific hypotheses, moral art tests values and rouses trustworthy feelings about the better and the worse in human action.

Given our usual embarrassment in the presence of words like "morality," this may seem a foolish way to speak about art. I hope to make it seem less so. I hope to explain why moral art and moral criticism are necessary and, in a democracy, essential; how it came about that the idea of moral art and criticism is generally dismissed by people who are in other respects intelligent and civil human beings; and what the right kinds of moral art and criticism are, or should be. Partly this involves explaining why sophisticated modern free society tends to be embarrassed by the whole idea of morality and by all its antique, Platonic- or scholastic-sounding manifestations—Beauty, Goodness, Truth; in other words, it involves explaining how false philosophers, and sometimes misunderstandings of true philosophers, have beclouded educated but sequacious minds, obscuring truths once widely acknowledged; and partly it involves sketching out a way of thinking that might supplant the Laodicean habits into which Americans have in recent times fallen.

I should mention immediately two nuisances with which my argument must deal. The first can be dispensed with quickly. It is a certain kind of artist's insistence that his art's morality is irrelevant, since he writes (or paints or composes) only for himself—to do anything else would be to aim at "the lowest common denominator," that is, ordinary humanity. The artist who feels contempt for most of humanity, and who works not out of love but out of scorn or ego or some other base motive, will be remembered down through time only insofar as his work, despite his theories, is admired and loved by the children of ordinary humanity. The writer may not care about any reader other than himself, but his work has no public existence except insofar as the feeling is not mutual. To say that one writes at least partly for others is not to say that one writes for everyone; one writes for people like oneself.

The second, more troublesome nuisance to be dealt with in an argument for moral art is that of treating justly the larger, to some extent secret morality of our time and culture—the invisible and largely unnoticed phantom morality which seems to be subtly, perhaps inexorably driving us toward the cliff. By this phantom morality I mean the basically decent and praiseworthy idea of the artist as fascinating freak; in other words, the atomist ideal, welcome in God but disastrous in human beings, of loving everything for itself alone. To attend exclusively to the individual or freakish can be to lose sight of what the freak has in common with all other living things: hope and the possibility of tragic failure.

Because this ideal, this celebration of the unique or

quirky, has so firmly taken hold in many quarters, the very notion of moral art seems to us, even on the level of feeling, paradoxical and unsettling. On the one hand we say (or used to say) that the artist should hold up ideals for imitation, he should inspire all humanity to certain qualities of action; on the other hand, the artist today is often considered interesting mainly for his oddity, or at the very least for his ability to spot and transmute into permanence the curious detail drawn from life or made up by fancy—the humpback's peculiar (real or imagined) way of scratching his back. It is moral and praiseworthy that we no longer scorn individuals who in outward form, personality, or character violate our reasonable and average expectations: that we no longer kill twins, that we no longer tie the left hands of naturally left-handed children behind their backs; that we can at last recognize as forgivably genetic the sometimes troubled nature of the XYY, a person who may be inclined by an accident of his conception toward disreputable behavior.

The widespread and growing feeling of sympathy for the freakish, the special, the physically and spiritually quirky, marks a huge advance in the quality of civilized, democratic life, and writers' passionate, unjudgmental examinations of the quirky have helped us make that advance; but one effect of the advance is that we begin to praise writers themselves for their oddity, not for their wisdom, universality, or even art. We praise the petty criminal Jean Genet at least partly because on certain narrow matters he's right, but also at least partly because everything he does is slightly shocking. We praise Beckett partly because his extraordinary despair is brilliantly dramatized and therefore "communicates," even though, at all his darkest jokes, the audience does not in secret cry out with tragic recognition, "Alas, that's true!" but only laughs with the recollection, "I remember one time when *I* felt as miserable as that." In Beckett the worst the universe can do becomes normative, and our worst impulses are made comically standard, while our best are shown to be ambiguous if not absurd. We laugh with decadent delight at the proofs, partly because Beckett is an authentic genius whose compassion and comic sense sharply undercut the nihilism, but we continue about our daily business—feeding our children, counting out honest change—as if they were false.

To worship the unique, the unaccountable and freaky, is—if we're consistent—to give up the right to say to our children, "Be good." To admire on the grounds of "unique personal vision" both Ivar the Boneless and England's King Alfred, one an obscenely savage monster even among Vikings, the other the first and last true Christian king, is at best morally audiculous (timorously audacious). Presumably, no fairminded reader will argue with that, at least when it's put in such black and white terms. There *is* something wrong with "snuff films," even if all the acting is excellent right up to the murder of the actress. But some questions remain. Just how serious is the need for moral criticism—since we all agree, after all, about snuff films? And what does the moral critic do with the perverse and disgusting but obviously sincere and well-intended work; that is, with the XYY piece of art?

Let me begin with some general remarks on how moral criticism has been justified in the past—justifications which once made such criticism standard.

As I've admitted already, *morality* has become, in many people's minds, an unattractive word, almost as unattractive as *criticism*. One could perhaps find a leaner, less obstreperous word; but the only thing wrong with *morality*, it seems to me, is that it's frequently been used as a means of oppression, a cover, in some quarters, for political tyranny, self-righteous brutality, hypocrisy, and failed imagination. One might as well turn against turnips because Sherman sometimes ate them in his march across the South. Let us say for the moment that morality means nothing more than doing what is unselfish, helpful, kind, and noble-hearted, and doing it with at least a reasonable expectation that in the long run as well as the short we won't be sorry for what we've done, whether or not it was against some petty human law. Moral action is action which affirms life. In this wide sense there is no inherent contradiction between looking with sympathetic curiosity at the unique and looking for general rules that promote human happiness.

It was once a quite common assumption that good books incline the reader to—in this wide and slightly optimistic sense—morality. It seems no longer a common or even defensible assumption, at least in literate circles, no doubt partly because the moral effect of art can so easily be gotten wrong, as Plato got it wrong in the *Republic*. To Plato it seemed that if a poet showed a good man performing a bad act, the poet's effect was corruption of the audience's morals. Aristotle agreed with Plato's notion that some things are moral and others not; agreed, too, that art should be moral; and went on to correct Plato's error. It's the total effect of an action that's moral or immoral, Aristotle pointed out. In other words, it's the *energeia*—the actualization of the potential which exists in character and situation—that gives us the poet's fix on good and evil; that is, dramatically demonstrates the moral laws, and the possibility of tragic waste, in the universe. It's a resoundingly clear answer, but it seems to have lost currency.

Various kinds of confusion creep in, for instance the objection that the universe *has* no moral laws—a false objection because it takes "universe" here to mean planets and stars, and not what we know the word does mean here—humanity grandiosely conceived. Or the objector imputes to us—because he was hurt by fundamentalist religion or else for love of obstruction for its own sake—imputes to us some medieval notion of God and his angels propelling things celestial around their Ptolemaic rings, giving man a harmonious model to imitate (concordant moral laws), and he demands—hissing at us, shaking his finger—that we show him an angel, one single live angel or his footprint. Worst of all, the objector looks into his heart and sees chaos there, and denies, forever after, that one mode of action is better than another for senseless, purposeless humanity. We see that we're mired in that old bog *L'etre et le néant*.

The annoying thing about discredited gospels is that they continue, though dead as doornails, to exert their effect. This is as true of philosophical mistakes as of bad theology. Except for the early books and the general thesis on human imperfectibility, most of Freud's thought has proved inadequate, yet we're all, to some extent, Freudians. Hard as they may smile, we doubt that our children really love us, or at least we keep watching for little proofs. And though Sartre's mistakes (as well as his right answers) are now fairly clear, almost no one dares return to the serious discussion of rational morality his outburst interrupted. Either there are real and inherent values, "eternal verities," as Faulkner said, which are prior to our individual existence, or there are not, and we're free to make them up, like Bluebeard, who reached, it seems, the existential decision that it's good to kill wives. If there *are* real values, and if those real values help sustain human life, then literature ought sometimes to mention them. But though Sartre's attack on eternal verities has at important points proved to be bad philosophy—we will con-

sider some of the mistakes a little later—serious talk
about art's moral center is as unfashionable today as
when he first began to kill the conversation with his
knowing smile.

Jean Paul Sartre was of course not the first to deny
that the values we must learn lie outside us; he was
perhaps original chiefly in rephrasing the atheistic and
absurdist arguments in the one metaphor surest to convince his moment: paranoia. But as the main or cur-
rently most commonly read advocate of that species of
thought against which Schopenhauer, Bradley, Collingwood, and Brand Blanchard, to name just a few,
complained, Sartre is a handy symbol of what has gone
wrong in modern thinking. Cut off from objective assessment of both naturalist hypotheses (values as implications of our mammalian and conscious nature) and
idealist hypotheses, especially notions of God and
(more important) rational goodness—cut off mainly, it
seems to me, because both were unfashionable in his
time and place—Sartre asserted, after some stylish but
no doubt sincere *angst,* a universe of whim, confusion,
and nausea, a universe where "the Other" is by definition the enemy, a universe he had, as Camus noticed,
projected mostly from inside.

Leo Tolstoy knew about the universe of despair and
endured a perhaps similar spiritual crisis, a crisis certainly profound and all-transforming. He came out of it
not with a theory that every man should make up his
own rules, asserting values for all men for all time, but
with a theory of submission, a theory which equally
emphasized freedom but argued that what a man ought
to do with his freedom is be quiet, look and listen, try
to feel out in his heart and bones what God requires of
him—as Levin does in *Anna Karenina,* or Pierre in *War
and Peace.* For God, if you wish, read "sympathy, empathy, scrupulous study of the everyday world and the

best men's books." Whereas Sartre invoked "the individual transcendent goal," the future as negation of the repellant present (what Bluebeard, being Bluebeard, decided one dark night he would make of himself, a murderer by rule), Tolstoy conceived a transcendent goal for humanity as a whole: like the earlier English and French Romantics, he envisioned a world ruled not by policemen but by moral choice, a world where every man's chief ambition was to be Christlike. Only through moral art, Tolstoy argued—or "religious art," as he preferred to say—can such a world be brought into existence.

Let me quote at some length Tolstoy's closing argument in "What Is Art?" for though we may not be as sure as Tolstoy that the Kingdom of God is nigh, the argument for moral art, and against so-called art that ridicules ideals, still seems to be correct, with or without its religious premise. Tolstoy writes:

The task of art is enormous. Through the influence of real art, aided by science, guided by religion, that peaceful co-operation of man which is now maintained by external means—by our law-courts, police, charitable institutions, factory inspection, and so forth—should be obtained by man's free and joyous activity. Art should cause violence to be set aside.

And it is only art that can accomplish this.

All that now, independently of the fear of violence and punishment, makes the social life of man possible (and already this is an enormous part of the order of our lives)—all this has been brought about by art. If by art it has been inculcated on people how they should treat religious objects, their parents, their children, their wives, their relations, strangers, foreigners; how to conduct themselves towards their elders, their superiors, towards those who suffer, towards their enemies, and towards animals; and if this has been obeyed through generations by millions of people, not only unenforced by any violence but so that the force of such customs can be shaken in no way but by means of art: then by art also other customs more in accord with the religious perception of our time may be evoked. If art has been able to convey the sentiment of reverence for images, the Eucharist, and for the king's person; of shame at betraying a comrade, devotion to a flag, the necessity of revenge for an insult, the need to sacrifice one's labor for the erection and adornment of churches, the duty of defending one's honor, or the glory of one's native land—then that same art can also evoke reverence for the dignity of every man and for the life of every animal; can make men ashamed of luxury, of violence, of revenge, or of using for their own pleasure that of which others are in need; can compel people freely, gladly, and spontaneously, to sacrifice themselves in the service of man.

The task for art to accomplish is to make that feeling of brotherhood and love of one's neighbor, now attained only by the best members of society, the customary feeling and the instinct of all men. By evoking under imaginary conditions the feeling of brotherhood and love, religious art will train men to experience those same feelings under similar circumstances in actual life; it will lay in the souls of men the rails along which the actions of those whom art thus educates will naturally pass.[1]

Some of Tolstoy's own late, didactic work—*The Resurrection*, for example—is not a good argument for this theory; but whatever the imperfections of some of Tolstoy's work, what he says here about "religious art" is true. Fairy tales change the lives of children, in ways Bruno Bettelheim has made an effort to explain in detail;[2] sympathetic black actors on TV have more power than busing laws; and the critics' veneration of the tragically neurotic self-pity and anger ("unflinching honesty") and, finally, suicide of Sylvia Plath is perhaps one of the reasons Ann Sexton is now dead.

No one seriously doubts, surely, that Tolstoy's essential argument is right: ideals expressed in art can effect behavior in the world, at least in some people some of the time. How the morality of the effect is derived, and how the process of improvement works, can be expressed in several ways, and though it doesn't really matter for my overall argument which of the various ways we choose, it will be worthwhile mentioning at least two of them, one grounded in a religious reading of the universe, the other not, or at any rate not of necessity. As proponents of the first view, let me mention, in chronologically disordered but convenient form, Tolstoy, Homer, and Dante.

Tolstoy argues, in effect—judging by his reviews, his comments on folktales, his novels, and his essay "What is Art?"[3]—that the ideal held up in a proper work of art comes from God, was originally revealed in action by the life of Christ the intermediary—it could be seen reflected, Tolstoy felt, in the lives of those who in his view most closely followed Christ's model, the best of the Russian peasantry in his day—and is passed on to all humanity by artists: first, he would say, by the direct recorders of Biblical events, then by the framers of folktales and parables of the sort Tolstoy collected in *The Flower Garden* and imitated in his own late fables, and finally by educated writers engaged in "religious art." Note the scheme: from God comes the standard; it is enacted by a hero and recorded by the poet.

With the worship of Zeus substituted for Christianity, this is almost exactly Homer's position, though the position is worked out in more detail by Homer—worked out, that is, in *The Iliad* and elaborated in *The Odyssey*. What the warrior-hero does on the battlefield, especially if he is half god, like Achilles, shows ordinary men what the gods love. (Despite their bickering, the gods, like men, desire order; this, Homer claims, is why Poseidon decides to give way to Zeus, his equal.) Sometimes the hero is directly possessed by the god and thus for a while *is* the god, as Achilles is possessed by Zeus during his purgatory rampage; at other times the gods trick the hero into serving as their image and model for mankind, as when Athena tricks Hector into standing and fighting for his doomed city instead of running. Every hero's proper function is to provide a noble image for men to be inspired and guided by in their own actions; that is, the hero's business is to reveal what the gods require and love, as do Hector and Achilles and those heroes still mightier of whom Nestor speaks. And whereas the hero's function (like the function of Tolstoy's Christ) is to set the standard in action, the business of the poet (or "memory" or "epic song," and also the business of arts other than poetry) is to celebrate the work of the hero, pass the image on, keep the heroic model of behavior fresh, generation on generation. This is the reason for Homer's emphasis on Hephaestus. As Zeus' fire possesses Achilles (daemonically entering him) and shows mankind a living image of how to behave when betrayals and general corruption must be purged, the artificer of the gods, Hephaestus, creates Achilles' shield in order to show forth in a picture what proper order ought to be; in other words, gives a visual image of the order to be pursued once the Iliadic evil is burned away. In the same way another, less perfect artist, Helen, names and describes the Achaean heroes so that Priam may "know them" and, more important, serves as pictorial historian of the war, preserving its battles as scenes on her loom. Nestor's role as moralist-historian is similar.[4]

The gods set ideals, heroes enact them, and artists or artist-historians preserve the image as a guide for man. It's the same in *The Odyssey*. When the court poet is driven from the palace of Agamemnon, Clytemnestra's betrayal is assured; as long as the poet remains in Odysseus' court, Penelope is relatively safe. The one important difference between the argument of *The Odyssey* and that of *The Iliad* is that in times of dangerous intrigue, the gods' model for man includes cunning and deceit, and at such times even poems—like Odysseus' stories—may craftily lie. This is a simplification of the total aesthetic argument in Homer, admittedly, but let it do for now. It is clear, at any rate, that for Homer—one way or another—art instructs.

Dante, too, believes truth comes from God, that it is expressed in action, here in the world, by some model figure, and that the poet's business is to capture the image of action and make it permanent through the power of art. Dante introduces profound complications, however: the model hero is Dante himself as he is influenced by the saintly intercessor, Beatrice. Both hero and heroine are human.

At its core, Dante's idea of moral art in *The Divine Comedy* may be described as more modern than Tolstoy's. Like Sartre at the time of his feeling of nausea, like Tolstoy at the time of his total doubt, Dante came to a period in his life when he realized he had utterly lost his way in a spiritual dark wood (the famous line admits also of a reading more grim: "abandoned my way"). Few men who have ever lived suffered greater *angst* than Dante, "one of the most tragic men known to history," an early biographer called him. Carlyle said of his portrait—reading it, of course, with Romantic fashion and Dante's poetry in mind—

I think it is the mournfulest face that ever was painted from reality; an altogether tragic, heart-affecting face. There is in it, as foundation of it, the softness, tenderness, gentle affection as of a child; but all this as if congealed into sharp contradiction, into abnegation, isolation, proud, hopeless pain.

For all the archaic flavor of Dante's allegory in the *Commedia,* both our relatively slight knowledge of his life and his own explicit (though sometimes conventional) statements in the *Commedia,* the *Vita Nuova,* and elsewhere make his exact situation clear: he had lost all sense of right and wrong (or at any rate all feeling for them), had no idea where to turn for help, and in his despair had hardly the strength to fight for survival, much less salvation.

It began, of course, with the death of Beatrice.[5] Dante tells us in his *Convivio* that after the death of Beatrice he sank into a deep and lasting depression, almost madness, and could find no consolation within or without. In imitation of Boethius, he says, he turned to the study of philosophy, making it his second "lady," and studying so hard that, for a time at least, he damaged his eyesight. In the *Convivio* Lady Philosophy comes off well, but this is generally considered a late reconstruction, and the truth (or else the earlier, truer metaphor) is probably closer to Dante's account in the *Vita Nuova*, where he describes his second love as faithless, accursed, and vile. William of Ockham was not yet born, but Dante's intellectual hero, Aquinas, had already confessed the severe limitation of logic, which, however rigorously applied, could support opposite conclusions. The poet was also deeply involved in the ugly world of Florentine politics, and there is some evidence that he sought to deaden his despair in a life of dissolution. His beloved fellow poet Guido Cavalcanti wrote a sonnet to him at about this time begging him to abandon base thoughts and evil companionship. Dante contracted such debts, probably in connection with his political activities, that his family was later constrained to sell estates to pay them off; he married a woman he did not love and in time seems to have come to hate; and he also contracted, during this period, tragic guilt. He could be something of a monster, a man who frequently returned evil for good, a vindictive neurotic who often failed to notice the pettiness, cruelty, and injustice of his own acts. But at times he did notice, and suffered greatly.

In the year 1300—the dark year in which the *Commedia* begins—Dante, as one of the priors of Florence, tried to establish peace in the city by banishing the most unruly chiefs of both parties, the Guelf and the Ghibelline. Motivated either by expediency and compromise or by his often ferocious idea of what was right—probably the latter—Dante had his friend Cavalcanti imprisoned at Sarzana, though his offense was slight. At Sarzana, Cavalcanti fell ill from the notoriously unhealthy climate and soon died. Whether or not it was his anguish at this that triggered the experience allegorized in the poem, Dante was deep in his "selva oscura." Reason, even religion, could not help.

Then one thing came to him: the image, memory, interior sensation of Beatrice. She alone was still real for him, still implied meaning in the world, and beauty. Her nature became his landmark—what Melville would call, with more sobriety than we can now muster, his Greenwich Standard.

Let us notice here two things. First, that Dante—steeped in the thought of Aquinas and already deeply versed in what remained of classical science and philosophy (Dante was, among other things, a medical doctor)—had by this time come to the same discovery Aquinas had reached: that logical argument can support opposite and mutually exclusive conclusions with equal force, so that reason is at best (like Virgil) a limited guide. Aquinas, abandoning his *Summa*, turned mystic. Temperamentally, devoted as he was to things physical and to the work of intellect, Dante could not easily take that route. Though we sometimes say, inexactly or perhaps metaphorically, that the *Commedia* is a mystic vision, it is of course nothing of the kind. The poem's construction is thoroughly intellectual (if we grant that poetic intuition plays a part in the work of intellect) and except for its traditionally derived images has nothing at all in common with mystic tradition.[6] Dante believed in God, it is true, and in his old age would prove profoundly religious; but it was the memory of Beatrice, not the thought of God directly, that stirred his emotions and enabled him to realize that something was still vital in him, that he might somehow find his way back to the road he had lost.

Second, it is interesting to notice that in his confusion and despair, Dante was in almost exactly Jean Paul Sartre's position, emotionally at least, at the time of Sartre's experience of nausea, and that he turned to a cure similar to Sartre's: he looked for value and meaning in his own history. Yet what could be more different than the result in the two cases! Finding life meaningless—drifting in a pointless and sickening universe, perceiving himself to be a brute "existent" without "essence"—Sartre sorted through his own life for pattern, any pattern, found certain casual structures there, and, having nothing else at hand, affirmed them as the purpose of his existence, later elaborating them into what amounts almost to a metaphysic. Sartre's program was undeniably a courageous and, in the ordinary sense, intelligent one. But the example of Bluebeard should give us pause. For years he has been, for one reason or another, killing off his wives. Now, finding his life disgusting, devoid of sense, he searches his experience for pattern, sees that he has regularly murdered his wives, and asserts that next time he will do it on purpose. *Voila!*

Dante's case is different. He hunts through his life and finds—or accidentally notices—one still vivid and liberating feeling: all that was summed up for him in the figure and mind of Beatrice. For Beatrice he felt (let us suppose) he would willingly live or die, as she should ask, since to him the choice no longer mattered. What *would* she ask? With a shock, he realized that he had discovered something like a new mode of thought. It was a mode to be rediscovered by the Romantic age, when the imagination was again to be liberated from the ferule of logic, this time the ferule of Cartesian and Newtonian rationalism. Dante would be the poet-hero of that age, and his discovery would be the essential Romantic method. Whatever logic might urge, Dante found, the fact was that to speak basely or wrongly before Beatrice filled him with shame—a crucial point he dramatizes in the closing cantos of the *Purgatorio* and through much of the *Paradiso*.

The *Commedia*, then, is Dante's construction of a complete universe, a total metaphysic presented as events and images (with, here and there, a syllogism), all built on the basis of one test—not at all, as some think, "What would Aquinas say?" (though Dante frequently follows Aquinas), but rather, "What can I say without shame or embarrassment, without a sense of being base or cynical, in the presence of Beatrice?" Most of us, I hope, have had some child or spouse or friend like Beatrice, someone who by his very nature, his seemingly innate goodness and intelligence, makes us uncomfortably conscious of our lies when we lie. Writers have been noticing and copying down such people for centuries—or making them up, if that can be believed. Literature abounds with these saintly figures—they need not be women or even young—and if the saints in some writers' fictions seem stick figures, like Dickens' Agnes in *David Copperfield* or Julien in Flaubert's *La légende de Saint Julien l'hospitalier*, that does not diminish Chaucer's Knight, Shakespeare's Ophelia, or a dozen heroes and heroines in the fictions of Henry James. Dante unquestionably believed that such people do exist, whether or not we today feel sure of it; and an unspoken premise in his way of thinking is that he himself, also, is capable of almost divine goodness, or at least sensitivity to goodness in others, Beatrice above all, his test of authenticity in himself.

His assumption is not the Platonic notion (the scheme in the *Symposium*) that his loved one can start him on the journey step by step up the ladder toward the good. He assumes that she *is* good, an incarnation of the divine principle. Love is a form of knowledge.

If we ask how could Dante, in his time of *angst,* come up with such a happy solution and Sartre, in his, come up with a solution so miserable, we can only say—given our modern (and Romantic) reluctance ever to lay blame—that Dante was deluded (Beatrice did not love him, or loved him but was actually promiscuous and a fool, or at best would in time have become less admirable and loving) or else that Sartre was psychologically unlucky. That may sound convincing, at first. Sartre's concept of "the Other" is invariably of the other who opposes or imposes or, if loved, flees. One of his typical ways of presenting the Other is his description of a man who, "moved by jealousy, curiosity, or vice," stands peeking through a keyhole. When the man hears footsteps in the hall behind him and knows he has been seen by some Other, the whole structure of his experience changes. Poor Sartre! we say, if we're philosophically naive. Sartre glances over at us and smiles. We will have to return, a little later, to that smile.

Homer, Dante, and Tolstoy derive art's morality from divine goodness. But morality as a principle of art need not be abandoned when the sky comes to be "ungoded." An alternative to the religious interpretation of the notion we've been treating—that ideals expressed in art can have an effect on people's behavior—is what we may describe as the Romantic and post-Romantic interpretation.

Whatever his Sunday devotions, and however conscious or unconscious he may have been of what he was up to, the Romantic artist took upon himself the labor of being everything at once: (1) the god who shapes the models for human behavior, (2) the heroic model (the equivalent of Christ, Achilles, or Dante as transformed by Beatrice's love), and (3) the singer of the hero's deeds. For the Romantic artist, generally speaking, it seemed that God did still exist—"almost certainly," he would say—but had grown in some ways exceedingly remote, was indeed becoming, as the nineteenth-century astronomer Laplace put it, a hypothesis of which the rational mind had no further need. Churches became suspect, though not valueless: they pressed for social change and gave nineteenth-century vicars time to work on their studies in philology. "God" became, for educated people, a hard word to swear by. Nevertheless, there was "something," though it might be no more than (as for Arnold) human love. One got from mountains, beautiful lakes, sometimes panthers, and most often from "the sad music of humanity," a general sense of, as Wordsworth expressed it,

> . . . something far more deeply interfused,
> Whose dwelling is the light of setting suns,
> And the round ocean and the living air,
> And the blue sky, and in the mind of man:
> A motion and a spirit that impels
> All thinking things, all objects of all thought.

Or, to put it in the more or less post-Romantic fashion of T. S. Eliot in the *Preludes* (before his conversion), one got from the world the sense of "some infinitely gentle, infinitely suffering thing." The change of tone is of course important, but the two affirmations are closer than they seem. Both are "religious," but they do not affirm that God exists, they merely express a lingering religious feeling. The absolute Good becomes not a bearded figure on a heavenly throne but an impression of what might be, an ardent wish. It was a wish worthy—for Shelley, among others—of martyrdom. We belong today to the same church, though the liturgy has changed. What is permanent for us is likely to be what it was for Wallace Stevens when he wrote,

> Beauty is momentary in the mind,
> The fitful tracing of a portal,
> But in the flesh it is immortal.*

God still exists, in other words, but we've swallowed him.

The Romantic poet or artist, because of his extraordinary sensitivity—his "exercized imagination," Shelley would explain (correctly, I think)—caught faint impressions of this Presence "out there" or within the human soul, or caught faint impressions of the total organization the Presence was and embraced, "the infinite SUM," as Coleridge says, and imitated in finite art the divine creative act. (We do the same except that for us, generally, "the divine creative act" is more emphatically metaphoric.) The Romantic thinker was not always ready for the language he would lead us to, language like that of Stevens; nevertheless, he could not comfortably say "God," since Rousseau and the Romantic fascination with the Greeks (especially saviors like Prometheus) had made the traditional stern and judgmental Christian God unpalatable.

What Rousseau had explained was that the misery and injustice of man's lot were not caused by a fall from grace but by bad human institutions. Thus humanity itself, innately good, became divinity enough, and the poet became its spokesman. (Hence, finally, Walt Whitman.) And so the Romantic poet looked into himself and at simple people around him and found there the implied model for individual and social action. That

*From Wallace Stevens, "Peter Quince at the Clavier," in *The Collected Poems of Wallace Stevens*. Copyright 1923 and renewed 1951 by Wallace Stevens. Reprinted by permission of Alfred A. Knopf, Inc.

model was not, Edgar Allan Poe believed, something the poet made up; it was an actual existent, source of "impressions" which the poet's art "conveyed." [7]

The optimism of the early Romantics was destined not to endure, at least in Europe, though it was basically right. Already by 1820, and certainly by 1848, after the failure of the French Revolution and the devastation of the Napoleonic wars, dejection—as in Coleridge's ode—was standard. It was not just kings who caused the trouble. Given power, the middle class, from which Romanticism had sprung, proved almost equally tyrannical, selfish, and dim-witted. An explanation was available in Romantic theory: the imagination, wellspring of compassion, was an innate faculty but one which required exercise and training. But in the heat of events—and in the din of individualist, anti-rational philosophies like Nietzsche's, wherein intuition serves not compassion and understanding but ferocious self-assertion, the Romantic hero as snarling Superman—the explanation went unheard.

As time has passed, the Romantic interpretation of how art does its work (the poet as divinity, hero, and singer) has been modified still more. Though a few late survivors of the Romantic age even now strike grand poses, most contemporary writers have abandoned the hopes and ideals of the Romantics—or pretend to have abandoned them. Most contemporary writers are hesitant to speak of Truth and Beauty, not to mention God—hesitant to speak of the goodness of man, or the future of the world—though they read *The Scientific American* and are uplifted or depressed by each new revelation about whether the universe is stabilizing or decaying. (Poets still believe, however shyly, in argument by analogy.) Most have the bearing not of Byronic heroes shouting on their cliffs but bespectacled professors who live by Robinson Crusoe's comfortable model of "due and regular conduct." There are old-style Romantics in South America and Kenya, but in the United States the Romantic interpretation is for the most part reduced to an unconfessed and sometimes loudly denied suspicion that art does indeed legislate for at least individual members of humanity. The novelist Stanley Elkin, for example, has proclaimed repeatedly that art is only art; but his fiction is forever urgently leading us—bullying us and his characters—toward what seems to Stanley Elkin the right way to live. The same bullying is patent in the work of E. L. Doctorow and, on a higher level, John Barth. One could name others, secret propagandists both good and bad, profound and ridiculous, for women's liberation, honesty in politics, sexual promiscuity—what have you. Few critics praise or attack what these propagandists say. A writer's truths, we tell ourselves, are matters of opinion.

But we are mistaken. However enfeebled the Romantic impulse on the one hand, or the religious premise of Tolstoy on the other, the moral position is still popular with writers, however loudly they may claim it's not so: art instructs. It's the same in all the arts. Nature follows craft, and the shrewd craftsman knows it. In the eighteenth century, people disliked nature (in the fourteenth century, for good reason, they disliked it even more); eighteenth-century gentlemen turned irrumpant nature to formal gardens, getting rid of all the mess, and if a painter had forests he couldn't dispense with, given his classical, allegorical subject, he browned away the garish green. By the nineteenth century, thanks to painters, poets, and musicians, everyone was gazing off the sea wall or traipsing through the woods.

Art instructs. Why, one may wonder, would anyone wish to deny a thing so obvious? We can safely assume in advance that a denial so widespread and earnest cannot come from simple meanness or stupidity. It is far more likely to rise out of a general change in our culture and self-awareness, perhaps a defect in our vision which is to some extent attendant on recent improvements in our vision. In societies as in individuals, after all, virtues and faults are very often flip sides of the same thing.

3

IF WE AGREE, at least tentatively, that art does instruct, and if we agree that not all instruction is equally valid—some people would persuade us to murder for kicks, some would urge us to treat all women as sex objects and all bankers as insensitive clods—then our quarrel with the moralist position on art comes down to this: we cannot wholeheartedly accept the religious version of the theory because we are uncomfortable with its first premise, God; and we cannot wholeheartedly accept the secular version of the theory because we're unconvinced that one man's intuition of truth can be proved better than another's. We are aware that our devotion to individual freedom, our anxiously optimistic praise of pluralistic society, since other societies are always unjust—hence our carefully nurtured willingness to sit still for almost anything—may tend toward the suicidal; but when we ask whom we should trust, we find ourselves, predictably, in the position Yeats described: "The best lack all conviction, while the worst / Are filled with passionate intensity." In the name of democracy, justice, and compassion, we abandon our right to believe, to debate, and to hunt down truth.

In a democratic society, where every individual opinion counts, and where nothing, finally, is left to some king or group of party elitists, art's incomparable ability to instruct, to make alternatives intellectually and emotionally clear, to spotlight falsehood, insincerity, foolishness—art's incomparable ability, that is, to make us understand—ought to be a force bringing people together, breaking down barriers of prejudice and ignorance, and holding up ideals worth pursuing. Literature in America does fulfill these functions some of the time—fulfills them more adequately, I suspect, than does the literature acceptable to the writers' union in Russia. But that makes the fact no less unfortunate that what we generally get in our books and films is bad instruction: escapist models or else moral evasiveness, or, worse, cynical attacks on traditional values such as honesty, love of country, marital fidelity, work, and moral courage. This is not to imply that such values are absolutes, too holy to attack. But it is dangerous to raise a generation that smiles at such values, or has never heard of them, or dismisses them with indignation, as if they were not relative goods but were absolute evils. The Jeffersonian assumption that truth will emerge where people are free to attack the false becomes empty theory if falsehood is suffered and obliged like an unwelcome—or, worse, an invited—guest. Yet to attack a work of fiction on moral grounds seems now almost unthinkable. Who but an ignoramus would disparage *Ada* because of Nabokov's merry, diabolical lie when he tells us our great charitable institutions were originally set up as whorehouses?

Part of the problem may lie, then, in an excessively timid idea of democracy. According to this view, the shoddy morality of much of our fiction reflects a failure to recognize and try to deal with the inexorable conflict at the heart of all free society, between the impulse toward social order and the impulse toward personal liberty. This conflict is sometimes described as a stereotypic class war—hard hats versus, say, college professors, or "the silent majority" versus the liberal. But actually the conflict is inside every one of us. On the one hand we prize and seek conformity. Keeping up with the Joneses means sharing their values, as TV commercials would persuade us to do (whiter teeth, softer hair), and if we tell the truth most of us, most of the time, are happy to be duped. On the other hand, we all feel the democrat's secret contempt for conformists and admire what we call "the individual," whether it be some such folk hero as Jessie James, the flim-flam man, the railroad bum, or the jewel thief, or whether it be the intellectual breakaway: Walt Whitman, Herman Melville.

In general, escapist fiction has always been conservative and conformist, serious fiction, individualistic. But there are signs that things are changing. As cynicism, despair, greed, sadism, and nihilism become increasingly chic, more and more meanness creeps into escapist fiction. Partly because, in reaction against stultifying conformity, we have learned not only not to scorn the moral freak but to praise him as somehow superior to ourselves, and partly because we have fallen into a commitment to sincerity rather than honesty (the one based on the moment's emotion, the other based on careful thought)—so that we admire more a poem which boldly faces and celebrates thoughts of suicide than we do a poem which makes up some convincing, life-supporting fiction—civilization has lost control of serious art.

What is involved is the age-old dilemma of the democratic optimist: distinguishing, as theologians put it, between the sinner and the sin or, in secular language, distinguishing individual dignity and worth from the individual's value (or lack of it) to the group. If we cannot make out what guilt is, virtue is academic. Few would deny that our humanness is enriched by our increasingly sophisticated notions of guilt and of society's part in the guilt of individuals; but if the moral artist is to function at all, he must guard against taking on more guilt than he deserves, treating himself and his society as guilty on principle. If everyone everywhere is guilty—and that seems to be our persuasion—then no models of goodness, for life or art, exist; moral art is a lie.

George Steiner points out in *The Death of Tragedy* that the Romantic vision "implied a radical critique of the notion of guilt." He continues:

In the Rousseauist mythology of conduct, a man could commit a crime either because his education had not taught him how to distinguish good and evil, or because he had been corrupted by society. Responsibility lay with his schooling or environment, for evil cannot be native to the soul. And because the individual is not wholly responsible, he cannot be wholly damned. Rousseauism closes the doors of hell.[8]

The Romantic opinion is of course still with us, partly because some of the time it is correct. Bad education and a desperate environment—for instance, the ghetto from which the most intelligent and "acceptable" tend to escape, leaving only the angriest, most frustrated, and helpless—have exactly the effect of immoral art, holding up bad models of behavior to the young and offering no convincing nobler models. A child made a transom thief at the age of five is wounded in a way that may hurt him all his life. The Kerner Commission report some years ago was informed by that truth, as was this country's decision to outlaw capital punishment; and if our sharply rising crime rate is to some extent a product of the Kerner report (since one effect of the report was a general reduction in sentences handed down to violent offenders) and also to some extent a product of our capital punishment law (if criminologists and law-enforcement officials are right that it encourages the murder of witnesses and hostages), the Rousseauist argument is nonetheless persuasive.

But the Rousseauist argument does not work in every case. Every month or so we read of some model child from an excellent school and family turning antisocial for no apparent reason. In fact, it is probably true of most of us that our civilized virtues run less deep than we would wish, and that given exactly the right turn of events or body chemistry we might turn criminal, might kill. In any event, the Romantic view will not explain away the tendencies of some people born XYY, and there may well be other genetic burdens that can incline us to destructive behavior. The Romantic theory improves our sense of justice, our concern for the underpriviledged, but in its optimism—its denial of life's potential for the tragic—it may well be sentimental. Though we struggle to deny it, and though only a madman would stare at it constantly, like Melville's Bartleby the Scrivener, life's potential for turning tragic is a fact of our existence. Drunken drivers do on occasion kill children; wars occasionally drive promising young men insane or snuff out their lives.

The Romantic attempt to evade tragic fact very quickly ran into trouble. Even where guilt has been defined out of existence, positive virtue sits uneasy. We notice three main attacks, those associated with the names Freud, Sartre, and Wittgenstein. Whereas the inescapable sorrow and bitterness of life—the fact that we die, that even children die—had for centuries been explained in the Western world as punishment for a fairly specific crime, the crime of Adam, or original sin, we learned from these three men a new kind of guilt—not really new, perhaps, but certainly never before so pervasive—the kind we call "free floating." This new kind of guilt, more terrible than the other, springs from the fact that, though one has done nothing particularly wrong, one cannot, by one's very nature, do anything of particular worth. It is the guilt of the metaphysically abandoned animal who, conceiving ideals beyond his nature, can only eat his heart out, self-condemned.

Consider what Freud, Sartre, and Wittgenstein would have done to our model moral artist, Dante. Freud, at least as he is popularly read, would have sought to persuade Dante that he did not really love Beatrice, nor she him. He saw in her an image of his mother, or of food: he transferred the physical gratification of suckling at his mother's breast, and his mother's sexual gratification and burden-relief, to the useful misconstruction "mutual love," and after the death of Beatrice, writing the greatest love poem in the world, he sublimated the brute emotions of hunger, loss, and rage against death as a father-facade in a way acceptable to his time and place, his superego.

Sartre, as it happens, has a wonderful passage on Dante and Beatrice, if we change Sartre's pronouns to proper names. When Dante was nineteen and Beatrice eighteen, both were virginal, God-fearing, upper-class Florentines well known for keen intelligence, but there were difficulties in the way of courtship and marriage. Dante and Beatrice are in conversation. Here is Sartre's scene, with the names of Dante and Beatrice slipped into it:

Beatrice knows very well the intentions which Dante cherishes regarding her. She knows also that it will be necessary sooner or later for her to make a decision. But she does not want to realize the urgency. . . . She does not apprehend Dante's conduct as an attempt to achieve what we call "the first approach"; that is, she does not want to see the possibilities of temporal development which Dante's conduct presents. She restricts this behavior to what is in the present; she does not wish to read in the phrases which he addresses to her anything other than their explicit meaning. If he says to her "I find you so attractive," she disarms this phrase of its sexual background; she attaches to the conversation and to the behavior of the speaker the immediate meanings, which she imagines as objective qualities. Dante appears to her sincere and respectful as the table is round or square, as the wall coloring is blue or gray. The qualities thus attached to the poet are in this way fixed in a permanence like that of things, which is no other than the projection of the strict present of the qualities into the temporal flux. This is because she does not quite know what she wants. She is profoundly aware of the desire which she inspires, but the desire cruel and naked would humiliate and horrify her. In order to satisfy her, there must be a feeling which is addressed wholly to her *personality*, i.e., to her full freedom—and which would be a recognition of her freedom. But at the same time this feeling must be wholly desire; that is, it must address itself to her body as object. This time then she refuses to apprehend the desire for what it is; she does not even give it a name; she recognizes it only to the extent that it transcends itself toward admiration, esteem, respect and that it is wholly absorbed in the more refined forms which it produces, to the extent of no longer figuring anymore as a sort of warmth and density. But then suppose Dante takes her hand. This act of her companion risks changing the situation by calling for an immediate decision. To leave the hand there is to consent in herself to flirt, to engage herself. To withdraw it is to break the troubled and unstable harmony which gives the hour its charm. The aim is to postpone the moment of decision as long as possible. We know what happens next. Beatrice leaves her hand there, but she *does not notice* that she is leaving it. She does not notice because it happens by chance that she is at this moment all intellect. She draws her companion up the most lofty regions of sentimental speculation; she speaks of Life, of her life, she shows herself in her essential aspect—a personality, a consciousness. And during this time the divorce of the body from the soul is accomplished; the hand rests inert between the warm hands of her companion—neither consenting nor refusing—a thing.[9]

810590

This, of course, is Sartre's celebrated description of "bad faith." We may agree that instances of bad faith do occur, and I'm willing to admit that in assigning Sartre's roles to Dante and Beatrice I am not being scrupulously fair; but we may nevertheless question whether bad faith is really an issue in the scene Sartre gives us. The most striking thing about Sartre's description is the harshness of its judgments, thus its falsity. Sartre's analysis of the woman's role makes her, literally, an autohypnotic. No such drastic explanation is required. Sartre's woman is simply, as we say, keeping her options open, casting nets toward several futures (to borrow another Sartrian phrase) and believing in all of them as tentative possibilities. When one of the possibilities matures, the rest will perhaps be forgotten, but right now, this moment, while she speaks of Life, she knows in the back of her mind what's happening to her hand. Sartre's trouble (except when he writes plays) is that he reads the world with a histrionic eye. Under extreme pressure the human psyche may indeed give way to "the lie in the soul," but the Sartrian habit of viewing all events from in front of the firing squad distorts reality. When we lack the requisite certainty for affirmation, it's through suspension of judgment—not *denial* of fact (bad faith)—that we grope from the present to the future. Surely when Dante first looked at Beatrice she did not say to herself, as Sartre seems to think she should have said, "He admires me and wants to go to bed with me." Out of such an experience as Sartre describes, the beginning of love as an act of "bad faith," Dante might, perhaps, have written the *Commedia*, but one doubts it.

Wittgenstein's program (and that of numerous positivists and analysts who have followed him) was as moral and humane as any ever conceived by a philosopher. Partly because of the general situation in Europe in his day—World War I, the rise of the Nazis, and World War II—he meant to demonstrate what Ockham and the nominalists had sought to demonstrate centuries earlier: that language is very tricky, that philosophy has a tendency to mislead, and that most of the connections philosophy makes are illusory, so that its work is, among other things, a bad excuse for killing people. Picking at language, at hidden metaphors and implied existents that aren't really there, he showed that most of traditional philosophy, certainly all metaphysics, tends not to stand up under close linguistic scrutiny. Philosophy, he showed, can rarely get to significant truth, though Truth may exist as "the inexpressible." At Dante's first words, *"Nel mezzo del cammin di nostra vita,"* Wittgenstein would interrupt politely, " '*Nel*' in exactly what sense?" Dante would never reach Paraidse at *that* pace. The poet might have answered—he did in fact answer, though Wittgenstein was still centuries from the light of the world—that only art can express the inexpressible. But hemmed in by doubters, confronted by men who claim (as Ockham would do, though the phrase is positivist) "one man cannot feel another's toothache," he would never have written the *Commedia;* he would have written, at best, the comic and ironic *Canterbury Tales.*[10]

We are beset, to an extent few people were before us, by doubts on every side; and the doubts are increased, if not partly introduced, by the moral relativism which naturally arises in a world of rapid communications and the sort of cultural interchange both invaluable and inescapable in the American melting pot. Values thought to be of prime importance prove trivial when one encounters an admirable culture in which those values are not held. Take language. It has been axiomatic with Anglo-Saxons for centuries that "cursing," as it used to be called, is strictly for people of base education and low moral character, pirates and murderers and the worst sorts of workmen on riverboats, people of whom it can repeatedly be said, "With a foul oath he. . . ." But when an American of Anglo-Saxon origin falls in love with a generous and high-minded, thoroughly decent black American who grew up in, say, one of the poorer neighborhoods of south Chicago, the Anglo-Saxon may be forced to discard that rule of "proper language" as transparently absurd. It is true enough that the upward mobility of the lower classes tends to clean up talk, but ever since the California Free Speech Movement we have understood that proper-language standards can be a form of social tyranny and the choice of "improper" language an expression of rebellion. The true artist is the one who—directly assisted by the techniques of his art, his art's mechanisms for helping him see clearly—can distinguish between conventional morality and that morality which tends to work for all people throughout the ages.

But here we face the greatest difficulty of all. It is an inescapable fact that a vast majority of the people on this planet live and die in abject misery and have always done so. How dare we claim that there is some "true morality" that could conceivably work for all people everywhere? John Fowles has addressed this difficulty in *Daniel Martin,* when his playwright scriptwriter hero ponders the question, How can a fortunate, happy man, living in the twentieth century, write a serious and authentic—that is, "tragic"—novel? Let me quote.

Even as Dan walked, he knew himself, partly in the very act of walking and knowing, and partly because of what had been happening during those last two weeks, dense with forebodings of a rich and happy year ahead. It was as ludicrous as that: forebodings of even greater happiness—as if he were condemned to comedy in an age without it . . . at least in its old, smiling, fundamentally optimistic form. He thought, for instance, revealing instance, how all through his writing life, both as a playwright and a scenarist, he had avoided the happy ending, as if it were somehow in bad taste. Even in the film being shot in California, which was essentially a comedy of misunderstandings, he had taken care to see hero and heroine went their separate ways at the end.

He was not wholly to blame, of course. No one, during all the script discussions about other matters, had ever suggested anything different for the close. They were all equally brainwashed, victims of the dominant and historically understandable heresy . . . that Anthony [a philosopher friend] had derided by beatifying Samuel Beckett. It had become offensive, in an intellectually privileged caste, to suggest publicly that anything might turn out well in this world. Even when things—largely because of the privilege—did in private actuality turn out well, one dared not say so artistically. It was like some new version of the Midas touch, with despair taking the place of gold. This despair might sometimes spring from a genuine metaphysical pessimism, or guilt, or empathy with the less fortunate. But far more often it came from a kind of statistical sensitivity (and so crossed into market research), since in a period of intense and universal increase in self-awareness, few could be happy with their lot.

Daniel Martin's conclusion, and evidently John Fowles', is the one inevitable for any true artist. He will tell in the novel he means to write—the novel we are reading—the truth, in effect Spinoza's truth, that outside civilization (privilege) we are nothing, mere battered brutes without choices, whereas inside, however unfair it may be, we have hope, including the hope that our good fortune may spread to others. Martin exclaims, "To hell with cultural fashion; to hell with elitist guilt; to hell with existentialist nausea; and above all, to hell with the imagined that does not say, not only in, but behind the images, the real."

The would-be artist who cannot tell moral truth from statistics, who cannot find "the real"—both in his images and behind them, as Fowles says—must inevitably wander lost in false questions of relativity.

The lost artist is not hard to spot. Either he puts all his money on texture—stunning effects, fraudulent and adventitious novelty, rant—or he puts all his money on some easily achieved or faked structure, some melodramatic opposition of bad and good which can by nature handle only trite ideas. One sort of artist can see only particular trees, the other only the vague blackish-green of the forest. The artist who gives all his energy to texture has no standard for judging the atoms or battling particulars of his work; he can say virtually nothing because his work consists wholly of nonessentials. The artist who ignores the specific qualities of his particulars (his character's Jewishness or Indianness, his flute note's timbre) can say only what everyone else says.

4

A PROPER BALANCE of detail and generality, the particular and the universal, is as crucial for the critic as for the artist, since critics go wrong in the same ways artists do. Some get caught up in the nonessential, creating useless categories, avoiding the real and important questions; others get so lost in their abstractions that they cannot catch qualifying details in a complicated work. Both mistakes do harm, but probably only the first needs comment, since it seems to be at present the more usual mistake, just as textural fiddling is the more usual—more fashionable—mistake of artists. Let me take, as an example of the critic caught up in nonessentials, the most popular kind of critic at the present time, the one whose chief interest is in distinguishing between the modern and the post-modern—by another formulation, the "conventional" and the "innovative."

Once one has observed that new modes have grown fashionable with writers, and one has therefore determined to distinguish between modernists and "post"-

modernists (since "modern" writers have already been defined, by the accident of their once having been called "modern," and these new writers are perceptibly different), one begins the work of filling up the categories. Writers like Faulkner and Hemingway proclaimed themselves truth seekers; how do postmodernists differ? With the question thus posed, it's natural to glance around and notice that some contemporary writers—the hardest ones to read and thus the easiest to teach—claim to be not very interested in "truth." "Aha!" the critic cries. "Post-modern!"

Actually, of course, some of those writers who disparage the pursuit of truth have merely grown wary of the word's potential for pretentiousness and moralistic tyranny; and many other contemporary writers, some of them good ones, are quite openly devoted to searching out truth, often by the use of highly innovative forms: Larry Woiwode, Mark Halpern, Guy Davenport, Grace Paley, Charles Johnson, and many more. But all this the hasty critic blinks: the advance guard has been sighted. A few significant writers, it seems, whether out of what John Fowles calls "elitist guilt" or for some other reason, no longer seek truth, or goodness or beauty, but address their talents to parody, to role-playing, to survival by "mythotherapy," as John Barth called it in an early work. The post-modern group is remarkably small, we discover, as an advance guard should be. Among academics, including those academics who write reviews for the *New York Times,* the *Los Angeles Times,* the *Washington Post,* and the *New York Review of Books,* it is a prominent group, as it is in courses on contemporary literature. But we may wonder if these people are really the ones who are writing (as the title of one anthology of their work suggests) the "fiction for the seventies." They may be not so much a group of post-modernists as a gang of absurdists and jubilant nihilists, and perhaps also a few morally concerned writers whose innovative methods got them trapped in the wrong room.

I am not denying that carefully designed categories are useful. We cannot reason about things but only about the names of things, as Hobbes pointed out— forever relegating writers of fiction to the ward of the unreasonable. Only with the help of carefully worked out categories can we tell what went wrong with tragedy after Shakespeare, or tell, even, which standard critical categories are misleading—"metaphysical poets," for instance. But when not used judiciously, critical eluctants illuminate certain things by darkening others. The aesthetic game-players identified with post-modernism do exist, juggling, obscenely giggling and gesturing in the wings while the play of life groans on; but for all their popularity with critics, reviewers, and certain kinds of readers, they are not necessarily the best or most intelligently representative writers of their moment. Identifying writers in terms of conventionality versus experiment, or concern about truth versus indifference, obscures what is central in all real art, what gives it its worth.

As true critics know, in every generation there are good artists and bad, and what chiefly distinguishes the one from the other is the true artist's faithfulness to his business, his profound though not necessarily conventional morality as confirmed by his writing, his test of what he thinks. All critical labels simplify, but those popular at the moment (and for the past several decades) are especially unfortunate because they separate out and discard as waste what is central. Some, like "conceptual art," evade or suppress the moral issue. Others, like "post-modernism," accidentally raise the issue of art's morality and take the wrong side.

The term "post-modernism" not only isolates a few

writers and praises them beyond their due, depressing the stock of others or willfully misreading them; it judges cynical or nihilistic writers as characteristic of the age, and therefore significant, and thus supports, even celebrates ideas no father would wittingly teach his children. Some critics deny this, claiming that "post-modern" is a descriptive, neutral term, not a term of praise, and in this they are sincere; but the writers they then talk about are invariably the "post-modern" ones—the writers the new term was invented to explain; moreover, in a world which values progress, "post-modern" in fact means *New! Improved!* When a contemporary writer, however young and vigorous, however wildly experimental, is identified because of his stodgy Faulknerian values as "modern"—that is, "old-fashioned"—not only that writer but the morality he defends is removed from serious discussion.

The true critic knows that badness in art has to do not with the artist's interest or lack of interest in "truth" but with his lack of truthfulness, the degree to which, for him, working at art is a morally indifferent act. And whether we look at latter-day modern or post-modern work, mediocre writing, painting, theater, and music is mostly what we find. The general badness may be partly an illusion, a phantasm conjured by purveyors and critics who, because of faulty theories on what makes art, bloat the reputations of mediocre artists and fail to appreciate the good ones who come their way. But good writers, good painters, or good composers of whom no one ever hears do not, in effect, exist; so that whether or not those good artists are out there, we are living, for all practical purposes, in an age of mediocre art.

Technically our novelists (for instance) are shrewd enough, and publishers and reviewers seem, as never before, eager to be of use. Nevertheless, wherever we look it's the same: commercial slickness, misplaced cleverness, posturing, wild floundering—dullness. Though not widely advertised, this is general knowledge. When one talks with editors of serious fiction, they all sound the same: they speak of their pleasure and satisfaction in their work, but more often than not the editor cannot think, under the moment's pressure, of a single contemporary writer he really enjoys reading. Some deny, even publicly, that any first-rate American novelists now exist. The ordinary reader has been saying that for years. Critics may still be enthusiastic—discovering new writers or discovering new depths in our established writers—but critics aren't exactly disinterested. Never judge the age of a horse by the smile of the farmer.

Though it's disguised by criticism concerned with the nonessential, the truth is that, in general at least, our serious fiction is not much good. The same is true of most of our Establishment-supported new music and nearly all of what passes for theater. Texture is king in all the arts.

Drama and styles of dramatic production come and go so fast one can hardly make use of examples when describing what's wrong—but something is wrong. There has been no first-rate drama on or off Broadway in years. I am discounting, under "first-rate," froth like *Sly Fox,* though we must later look into the question of why we in America can do trivia so extraordinarily well—why our cinematography is so far ahead of our cinema, why the sets and timing in our musicals are so good when all of our recent musicals are so abysmal, why our thriller writers are often superior to our would-be serious artists except when, like Ross MacDonald, they're talked into trying to be artists. And in claiming we have no first-rate theater I'm also discounting the occasional good piece imported from, especially, Eastern Europe, where drama is, at its best, as healthy as it has ever been. As of this writing, what remains when we've discounted the froth and the best imported work is largely drama not worth sitting through.

We get plays brilliantly staged and performed but not carefully thought out by the playwright or director, like *Equus* and *The Comedians,* plays which, under scrutiny, collapse in philosophical and moral confusion. We encounter exceptions, for instance Edward Albee's *Zoo Story,* some years ago, or *Who's Afraid of Virginia Woolf?;* but even here, in the best of Albee's plays, we catch, I think, hints of the propagandistic falsification which first took center stage in *The Death of Bessie Smith,* hints of the unhealthy fascination with ugliness and pain that will later become Albee trademarks, and hints of that hollow profundity we find in much of Albee's later work, as in so much recent fiction. Or one might advocate, as exceptions, the quasi-philosophical entertainments of Tom Stoppard—notably *Rosencranz and Guildenstern Are Dead, Jumpers,* and *Travesties*—but even at his best Stoppard evades concern. The plays have no conclusions, and in fact from the outset the existential accidents on which the thought of the plays depends are so obviously contrived, like the too-easily manipulated elements of a farce, that we're discouraged from expecting more than a theatrical finale. Not, of course, that comedy and absurdity can never lead to anything serious—as Stoppard shows, himself. The accident of George Moore's carrying, in *Jumpers,* the name of a more famous philosopher, and also his accidental murder of his tortoise—these raise questions Stoppard makes serious for us even as we laugh. But the tone, the ultra-theatrical pizzazz, the delightfully flashy language which is Stoppard's special gift—all these warn us in advance that the treatment of ideas is likely to be more fashionable than earnest-predictable talk about the meaninglessness of things, the impossibility of "knowing," and so on. Stoppard's plays are considerably better than most, but disappointing: they raise intellectual and emotional expectations, then abandon us. From lesser writers we get plays far less interesting—at worst, last year's *Brief Lives,* a masterful one-man show except that nothing but the set and the actor's skill held interest, a comedy at which no one laughed except (a) when the character filled his cup too full, spilling a little, and (b) once when he pissed on stage.

Years of such bad or disappointing theater, over-praised by critics on the grounds that legitimate theater needs support, have led to the emergence of a new style in theater direction, both for entertainments and for more serious art, what might be described as the back-field-in-motion play. Most productions, these days, are marred by a continual agitation of the actors, a pointless clamor for attention by everyone onstage. The 1976–77 Lincoln Center production of *The Threepenny Opera* offends in this way. Tempos are rushed from beginning to end, so that only those in front can catch more than a few words; and no matter who's singing, no matter what the mood, one or more actors are seen rushing around dancing, arresting people, monkeying with the set. Even in *Porgy and Bess* the direction calls for continual motion, excessive monkeying and mugging. The message in such productions is clear: never mind the play, never mind the music or language or the sad humanity of the audience. For dramatic art—character and action, *energeia* leading to emotion and thought—directors are substituting football, stock-car racing, and sometimes hell-fire preaching. They imagine that they must trumpet the "ideas" in Shakespeare or that Euripides is made more interesting by directional effects like sheep guts and screaming. And then there are the softer, more "aesthetic" directors who go for the effete dance, who at auditions for a Shakespearean play ask actors and actresses to imitate a washing machine, a motion-picture projector, a limp asparagus, and who never ask them to read a line.

The superficiality of so much contemporary theater seems to come not just from timidity and foolishness but also, to some extent, from theory. Motion, glitter—texture for its own sake—has come to be the central value in the arts. Western civilization has been through this before, in the early Middle Ages, when the message of a work of art was fixed (love charity, shun carnality) and the orthodox poet had only the surface of his work to manipulate, decorating message with the colors of rhetoric, hunting out new tricks of texture, gauding, enameling, gilding. The problem today is not that the meaning of our works is fixed (so that we're free to pour our energy into ornament, as in the *Books of Kells*) but that we tend to feel we have nothing to say—or nothing to offer but well-intentioned propaganda—so we keep ourselves occupied with surfaces.

The subversion of art to the purposes of propaganda leads inevitably to one or the other of the two common mistakes in bad art: overemphasis of texture on the one hand, and manipulative structure on the other. Where characters are stick figures—cartoons of good and evil—and where plot is kept minimal and controlled by message, not by the developing will of lifelike human beings, the playwright has nothing at his disposal but the set and his caricatures' talk. Hence the bombast of a play like Baraka's *Dutchman* or Ed Bullins' push toward the ultimate textural surprise, the murder of a member of the audience.

Even our best or at least most serious playwrights

lean excessively on the methods of propaganda. Edward Albee's new play, *Listening,* is an example. In the radio version, designed, apparently, for transfer to the stage, the play's only physical action, aside from the entrance of the play's three characters, is that of a character who slashes her wrists because no one will listen to her. The message is the evil of manipulation, and to express it Albee purposely manipulates his audience, frustrating its reasonable wish to know who the characters are, whether they are alive or dead, where they have met, and what it is that they are talking about. Thus he preaches the evils of manipulation not by drama but by insult and coercion, techniques more appropriate to the tyrant than to the artist. Allowing himself only minimal use of plot, character, or even intellectual argument, and choosing to make very little use of setting, Albee depends almost entirely on random-sounding sentences. Odd and innovative as it may seem at first glance, the play is thus typical of present theatrical art: all texture. Texture is our refuge, the one thing we know we're good at. This is perhaps one reason ballet is now the healthiest of the arts. Here a failure of surface means total failure, as it does not in fiction, symphonic music, or even painting.

Contemporary music is generally as uninteresting as contemporary theater, though a change is in the wind. The hip composer's fascination with surface reveals itself in a number of ways; for instance, in obsessive concern with the shape of the isolated note. The musician plays a note. We listen. He stops. He plays another note. Such music may have, for the beginning listener, some very slight educationl value; but the idea that we have to be taught to listen to individual notes is preposterous to anyone who has ever spent time practicing an instrument. Another form of this textural obsession has been evident, ever since John Cage began to theorize, in the hip composer's use of noise and chance, even non-notation and the non-repeatable performance. (Compare conceptual and self-destruct painting and sculpture.) Without some form of Cage's theory, the Beatles might conceivably never have made "A Day in the Life" and the operatic use of noise as music might have stopped with Siegfried's banging on his sword. But the fact remains that individual sounds and non-conventional sounds—old, new, weird, worried, lumped, lambasted, bent, blasted, buttery, bopped, meeped, or moaned—are mere sounds, mere surface, boring or annoying, like the waste in this sentence, if not used for some purpose, transmuted by context.

The morality of music is faithfulness to the immutable laws of musical gravity (the laws by which melody tends to fall and progressions sink to resolution and rest) and faithfulness to the particular work's emotional energy; that is, for instance, the power and thrust of an ascending scale, a blast of trumpets, a crash of drums, a flute note. Great music pushes upward, soars, sinks, fights, and at last gives in or fails or wins or accepts, in sorrow or triumph, with a comic burp, or in some other of its infinite ways. Its devices are inexhaustible, vastly beyond capture in any theory of composition, though a theory book helps. But infinite as music's devices may be, its failures are all alike: even after we have listened carefully again and again, we do not like—that is, *believe*—the music. The emotion generating the music is fake, or secondhand, or feeble. The performer, not the composer, may be at fault; but whatever the cause, music goes wrong as any other dramatic development goes wrong. Honest feeling has been replaced by needless screaming, pompous foolishness, self-centered repetitiousness, misuse of the vocabulary.

Obviously, feeling can come either from texture or

from structure—two muted violins do not suggest the same emotion as does a choir of trombones—but structure also carries feeling, as we see beyond doubt when we follow a progression of musical events or, still more baldly, when a familiar melody comes back. And in music as elsewhere, structure, not texture, is primary, though it cannot stand alone. Bach's *Toccata and Fugue* is about equally successful played on an organ or played by a symphony orchestra and might even be successful transposed to a new key, as Bach frequently transposed his work for some new combination of instruments. If we are annoyed when it is played on a Moog synthesizer the reason is only partly textural. The electronic sound is unsubtle in the extreme, raising wrong connotations (comic and mechanistic). But a greater part of the reason for our annoyance has to do with structure. The synthesizer kills dynamics, smashes through nuances, and equalizes the music's progression of events so that we can feel no dramatic profluence.

From what I have said, my objection to the presently fashionable schools of contemporary music (except for the rising school of neo-Romantics and neo-classicists, who make only occasional and sparing use of music's more extravagant new devices) should be obvious. I object to the limitations of electronic music, though not to its existence as one more available device. I object to most (but not all) chance music because it is, usually, just circus: if it is successful on some particular occasion the reason is likely to be pure luck (and luck has no significant role in moral act, affirming nothing) or else the success hints at what some performer might have done with more interesting materials. One of the most popular forms of chance music at the moment is random-fragment music, as when, for instance, each section of the orchestra has a card containing two or three short motives to be played at any tempo or dynamic level, either with or without a signal from the conductor. (The card may contain, instead, pictures of Abraham Lincoln, Mount Everest, and a banana.) All one can really say about such works is, if the musicians enjoy them, let them play them—actually, most musicians hate such things—but let no one mistake what is happening for music: it's sport. God knows what kind of activity we're engaged in when for forty-five minutes two cellos play a perfect fifth. (Asked by the composer what he thought of this piece, an older and wiser composer quipped, "Just as I was beginning to get interested, it stopped.")

The worst that goes on in our music, however, is not electronic, aleatory, or otherwise "experimental" but relatively conventional music indifferent to art's immutable law of more or less balanced sensation and idea, and it is this music that shows us most clearly what is wrong. Some of our new music is cold-blooded, theoretical, following the directions worked out by Boulez and Babbett. At the other extreme we get brawling but imprecise emotion, what I earlier called "feeling unabstracted," music written in indifference to the simple principle: figure out what peak you're going for and go there. Not that I attack dissonance or noise or even the disintegration of music, as in Sibelius' Fourth Symphony. What I object to is noise without structural justification. Listening to music that rambles, poking around, hoping something may turn up—a quality acceptable only in the beginning composer's first draft—is like tracing the meanderings of an inept novelist, one who, say, mindlessly follows the uneventful life of some drugged rock-guitar player, hoping that sooner or later he will fall in love or be run over by a truck. Both failures, the cold-blooded and the gushingly mindless, stem from ignorance of how music imitates—or rather translates—reality.

As the laws of nature, working with all the materials of the universe, make a gorilla or a day lily, the composer, working with notes, makes a sonata. The sonata is not an imitation of some actual gorilla or day lily but a creation parallel, in its principles of vitality and growth, to the animal or plant, hence a new object under the sun. (This does not make the sonata—as William Gass might maintain—no more significant than a natural object. The sonata is, after all, man-made.) It is true that a tone poem like Sibelius' *Tapiola,* or a symphony by Mahler or Beethoven, may also imitate something in nature or legend, just as a ballerina may imitate a swan; but in this case, the composer has set for himself a double goal, not only imitation of nature's process but also imitation of some particular natural thing. In great art process-imitation is always primary. As nature creates, the composer creates. The resulting thunderstorm must be as inevitable, by strict laws, in the concert hall as it is on the mountain. In texture alone there *is* no process; there is only effect.

Literature has been suffering in a similar way. For years fiction has been generally unsatisfying. It may seem at first glance that no single cause is behind the badness—that things are just bad, there's some befuddlement in the air, a different befuddlement in the case of each writer. But I think if we analyze what leaves us dissatisfied in the work of each writer, one single cause does in fact emerge. In literature, structure is the evolving sequence of dramatized events tending toward understanding and assertion; that is, toward some meticulously qualified belief. What we see around us is, for the most part, dramatization without belief or else opinion untested by honest drama. William

Gaddis has named the problem in *JR*, though he himself doesn't escape it: "believing and shitting are two different things."

On the whole, our serious novelists, like our painters and composers, are short on significant belief. Though quick to preach causes of one sort or another, and quick to believe slogans, including literary slogans, they're short on moral fiber—the special moral fiber, part character, part knowledge, of the artist. Some, detached from life as by a wall of glass (Camus' image)—detached from real emotion by their cool, fashionable, but wrong conceptions—can muster up no feeling for either Red Riding Hood or the Wolf, only for literary form, art's devices, the proper definition of *hysteron proteron*. Some, though as earnest as St. Peter on the cross, or as Jacques Lipchitz sculpting his huddled masses, have no feeling for art's method, no faith in art's ability to lead the artist to discovery—the real, little-understood "technique" of fiction—so they allow the Wolf to eat Red Riding Hood alive, though a single phrase inevitable from the beginning could have saved her. Insofar as literature is a telling of new stories, literature has been "exhausted" for centuries; but insofar as literature tells archetypal stories in an attempt to understand once more their truth—translate their wisdom for another generation—literature will be exhausted only when we all, in our foolish arrogance, abandon it.

Since literature is by far the most accessible of the arts, both because it is the most explicit in its vocabulary and because it is the one art available to everyone, from Miami to Montana, this is the ideal test case. How well are our best writers likely to hold up?

They will not hold up, surely, if their works lack conviction, and conviction is a quality many contemporary writers avoid on principle. William Gass, professional philosopher and celebrated author of *Omensetter's*

Luck, the short story collection *In the Heart of the Heart of the Country, Willie Master's Lonesome Wife,* and a "philosophical inquiry" *On Being Blue,* maintains in his essays and tries to prove in his fiction that writers can use words only in the way logical positivists do, as intellectual concepts or gallaxies of concepts, so that to think of a character as a "real person" is naive: characters are merely verbal structures. I will argue with that later; for now let me simply remark that Kenneth Burke could easily answer Gass with his wise distinction between "action" and "motion"—the world of consciousness (action) as an emotional and symbolic translation of the world of brute force (motion). All our language, all our thought and opinion, all our deeply felt symbolism, Burke reminds us, comes from the world of things, the world of bumping atoms, thoughtless squirrels and trucks, so that before we can get to the great idea *True,* an emotionally charged symbolic construct for which innumerable women and men have died, we must first stare thoughtfully and long at a *tree,* Old English *trēow,* which gave us the word *true* (*trēow*), the "deeply rooted" idea. Some words may in the fullness of time become almost pure concept, nearly devoid of charge, like the word *square root* (from vulgar Latin *ex quadra,* "made from four," and *root* as in raddish), but it is a painful fact of the world of action, as of the world of motion, that nothing stands firm, eternally endures: as sure as nature is never spent, some poet will come along and use *square root* in a metaphor hinting at what is central in anger, or pain, or love, changing it forever.

Every word, even the dullest and most frivolous, makes waves, calls up dark, half-unconscious associations which poetic context can illuminate (all conscious life, Kenneth Burke would say, is poetic context), so that despite Gass' theory, when we read Gass' fiction, especially his early fiction, we see not merely textures but people eating breakfast; that is to say, we intuit what Wittgenstein rightly denied to systematic thought but allowed to poetry in his image of the ladder, "the inexpressible." Every metaphor conjures an inexpressible but felt background, ties the imagined to the fully experienced. Consider how meaning ripples out in, for instance, the line: "He raised his hand slowly and waved good-bye like a child erasing a blackboard." Or from Gass himself, "Drafts cruise through the room like fish." One can block this effect of language, and in his later books Gass sometimes does; but it is a real and common effect. With each book he writes, persistently urging his philosophical dogma—the assertion that *fish* means, simply, "fish," not the smells, shapes, cultures, with their emotional attachments, in which fish occur (or in Gass' line above, the limited set of shapes and colors, the implied bowl in which the fish occur)— refusing to submit to the artist's humble business, service of the muses—refusing, that is, *ecstasy* ("self-denial," hence "abandonment of willful control," "surrender to the fictional material's demands")—Gass more stridently argues his theory, and we are shown more clearly what a paltry thing is fiction designed to prove a theory. He presents, when he likes, magnificently vivid characters and scenes, the kinds of materials that engage both the reader's emotion and intellect; that is, revitalize the reader's consciousness, reminding him of how it feels to stand in an orchard or, say, a large old house. Then, indifferent to the miracle he's wrought and determined to prove that the energy is the same, Gass shifts to mere language—puns, rhymes, tortuously constructed barrages of verbiage with the words so crushed together that they do indeed become opaque as stones, not windows that allow us to see thoughts or events but walls where windows ought to be, richly textured impediments to light. In *Willie*

Master's Lonesome Wife, he creates a character, then tells us, in the character's voice, that the character is only words, she does not exist. One indication that his theory is faulty is our annoyance at the betrayal. We know that the writer, not the character, has made the statement. After working for a while within fiction's old conventions, he has broken the rules, quit the game like a sorehead when he's the only pitcher we've got.

Fiction as pure language (texture over structure) is *in*. It is one common manifestation of what is being called "post-modernism." At bottom the mistake is a matter of morality, at least in the sense that it shows, on the writer's part, a lack of concern. To people who care about events and ideas and thus, necessarily, about the clear and efficient statement of both, linguistic opacity suggests indifference to the needs and wishes of the reader and to whatever ideas may be buried under all that brush. And since one reason we read fiction is our hope that we will be moved by it, finding characters we can enjoy and sympathize with, an academic striving for opacity suggests, if not misanthropy, a perversity or shallowness that no reader would tolerate except if he is one of those poor milktoast innocents who timidly accept violation of their feelings from a habit of supposing they must be missing something, or one of those arrogant donzels who chuckle at things obscure because their enjoyment proves to them that they are not like lesser mortals. Where language is of primary concern to the writer, communication is necessarily secondary. Gass is handy proof. He begins his philosophical-poetic essay *On Being Blue* as follows.

Blue pencils, blue noses, blue movies, laws, blue legs and stockings, the language of birds, bees, and flowers as sung by longshoremen, that lead-like look the skin has when affected by cold, contusion, sickness, fear; the rotten rum or gin they call blue ruin and the blue devils of its delirium; Russian cats and oysters, a withheld or imprisoned breath, the blue they say that diamonds have, deep holes in the ocean and the blazers which English athletes earn that gentlemen may wear; afflictions of the spirit—dumps, mopes, Mondays—all that's dismal—low-down gloomy music, Nova Scotians, cyanosis, hair rinse, bluing, bleach; the rare blue dahlia like that blue moon shrewd things happen only once in, or the call for trumps in whist (but who remembers whist or what the death of unplayed games is like?), and correspondingly the flag, Blue Peter, which is our signal for getting under way; a swift pitch, Confederate money, the shaded slopes of clouds and mountains, and so the constantly increasing absentness of Heaven (*ins Blaue hinein,* the Germans say), consequently the color of everything that's empty: blue bottles, bank accounts, and compliments, for instance, or, when the sky's turned turtle, the blue-green bleat of ocean (both the same), and, when in Hell, its neatly landscaped rows of concrete huts and gas-blue flames; social registers, examination booklets, blue bloods, balls, and bonnets, beards, coats, collars, chips, and cheese . . . the pedantic, indecent and censorious . . . watered twilight, sour sea: through a scrambling of accidents, blue has become their color, just as it's stood for fidelity.

No one will deny that the writing is beautiful; we ask only that we not get much more of the same. You must take my word for it that Gass does not move from this to translucency; on the contrary, he continues in the same way for pages and pages. (In music, painting, theater, and poetry this kind of thing is sometimes praised as "circuit overload." No one has yet satisfactorily explained why in troubled times we should overload our circuits.) Gass is not alone, though he's the best of the lot, or at least the most stubbornly unreadable and thus most widely read by students and professors who admire opacity. Mobs of contemporary writers—writers very different in other respects—follow Gass in focusing their attention on language, gathering nouns and verbs the way a crow collects paper clips, sending off their characters and action to take a long nap. J. P. Dunleavy, Ron Sukenick, James Purdy, Stanley Elkin, John Barth, and a good many more of our writers concentrate, to a greater or lesser extent, on language for its own sake, more in love, on principle, with the sound of words—or with newfangledness—than with creating fictional worlds. One might say, in their defense, that what they create is "linguistic sculpture," or one might argue that some of this tightly wedged, cockleburred fiction goes beautifully, like *Finnegans Wake,* when read aloud. (Even about *Wake* one may, of course, have reservations.) But the fact remains that the search for opacity has little to do with the age-old search for understanding and affirmation. Linguistic sculpture at best makes only the affirmation sandcastles make, that it is pleasant to make things or look at things made, better to be alive than dead.

The more time one spends piling up words, the less often one needs to move from point to point, argument to argument, or event to event; that is, the less need one has of structure. Many people now working at serious literature do move in neat, episodic form from point to point, notably the so-called moderns, sometimes called writers of the "liberal tradition"; that is, writers concerned with discovering and passing on the values of a free society; and it is natural to expect of these writers a greater engagement with life's burning issues. But on the whole, we discover, even writers who profess a concern about truth do not often take the trouble to search out real understanding or dramatically earn their assertions. The modernist's truth tends to be not responsible and judicious, but just fashionable. Instead of the decadence of texture without structure, the enfeebled modernist offers structure independent of—and indifferent to—texture. Often, for example, the fiction's characters have no effect on the plot because the writer is all but unaware of their existence. Though they wail and howl and take cyanide, their creator, like the God of the Calvinists, loves only his ideas. Universals run roughshod over the particulars they require for validation. This decadence is in a way even less to be admired than the decadence of opaque language. Instead of saying nothing, it says, with speciously dramatic effect, fashionable things that are not so.

5

WHAT has gone wrong? Why is it that even those of our writers who insist that they care about argument are for the most part incapable of constructing an argument that will hold?

Perhaps the answer is too obvious for general notice. Love is knowledge, Dante discovered. Hate may also be knowledge of a kind—it peoples Dante's Hell—but Dante hates that which opposes what he loves.

To some of our best-known modernists, outrage is more appealing than are careful exploration and persuasion, for which the fuel can only be concern. For all the power of her journalistic writing, and for all the true feeling in some passages of her fiction, Joan Didion's novels, *Play It As It Lays* and *A Book of Common Prayer*, present, too often, fashionably pained characters who express fashionable opinions and black peeves. Insofar as we're unable to care about the characters, we can work up no interest in the issues; or if we do care about the ideas, it is only because we feel obliged to, and we accept the writer's value judgments for the same bad reason. To take another example, though Walker Percy is capable of writing fairly interesting novels like *The Moviegoer,* he is capable of descending, as in *Lancelot,* to sententious rehashing of ideas out of Nietzsche and Dostoevsky on the moral outsider (this time a despicable one), adding nothing personal but his Catholic anxiety and his scorn of people he dislikes. Harry Crews, like many a renegade fundamentalist, slams away, on and on, at those much picked-on villains, uneducated and unsophisticated Southerners, the same people Anne Tyler selects for her novels and, having more charity in her religion, presents as partly admirable human beings. Harry Crewses are at least as common as Anne Tylers. Too often we find in contemporary fiction not true morality, which requires sympathy and responsible judgment, but some fierce ethic which, under closer inspection, turns out to be some parochial group's manners and habitual prejudices elevated to the status of ethical imperatives, axioms for which bigotry or hate, not love, is the premise.

Nothing about the present situation in the arts is more curious than the fact that injust writers are quite regularly praised, whether they write in old-fashioned form, as Harry Crews does, or in more innovative form. Consider Robert Coover's much-anthologized short story "A Pedestrian Accident."

The story tells of a young man named Paul who has been run over by a truck. A callous crowd gathers to enjoy the spectacle, the callous truck driver noisily defends his own innocence in the matter, a horrible old woman named Mrs. Grundy, taking advantage of Paul's inability to speak, tells lies about her sexual relations with him, to the crowd's cruel delight. Three authority figures lend their efforts: a policeman who can get nothing done, a physician whose only contribution is to get the truck driver to move his truck, running over Paul again, then put it back where it was, and a priest (or so Paul at first thinks) who turns out to be a bum who is waiting for Paul to die and have no need of his clothes. In style the story imitates slapstick movie comedy, except that everything is obscene, everything mocks the values and hopes of Christianity, everything is cruel, and nothing is really funny or meant to be. The policeman asks Mrs. Grundy her name. This is what follows.

"Mrs. Grundy, dear boy, who did you think I was?" She patted the policeman's thin cheek, tweaked his nose. "But you can call me Charity, handsome!" The policeman blushed. She twiddled her index finger in his little moustache. "Kootchy-kootchy-koo!" There was a roar of laughter from the crowd.

The policeman sneezed. "Please!" he protested.

Mrs. Grundy curtsied and stooped to unzip the officer's fly. "Hello! Anybody home!"

"Stop that!" squeaked the policeman through the thunderous laughter and applause. Strange, thought Paul, how much I'm enjoying this.

This kind of thing goes on and on, with a tiresome effect that is seemingly intentional, a formal expression of the worldview, weariness and anger. At the end of the story a dog runs off with a piece of Paul's flesh, the bum waits on, and Paul lies in the rain awaiting death. Coover writes:

For an instant, the earth upended again, and Paul found himself hung on the street, a target for the millions of raindarts somebody out in the night was throwing at him. There's nobody out there, he reminded himself, and that set the earth right again. The beggar spat. Paul shielded his eyes from the rain with his lids. He thought he heard other dogs. How much longer must this go on? he wondered. How much longer?

The scene is of course an ironic crucifixion: when the earth upends, Paul hangs on the street as on a cross. The tone is the bitter irony of an apostate fundamentalist: "There's nobody out there, he reminded himself, and that *set the earth right again.*" Paul's assertion (and Coover's) that "There's nobody out there" is of course no more provable, except by faith, than the contrary assertion of Coover's Baptist-country childhood, and in fairness we must admit that the Baptist assertion brought with it, at least, the goals, if not always the practice, of responsibility, brotherhood, and love. Perhaps because practice is always faulty, and Coover is an idealist, Coover angrily mocks the whole Christian way of thinking. I doubt that anyone would seriously maintain that the world is as Coover says it is; yet the story is repeatedly anthologized and taught. The reason, surely, is not solely that the story is "innovative" and not that the argument against the Christian world view seems persuasive. It is rather that readers of a certain kind take pleasure in attacks on Christendom, and the more outrageous the attack the better. Readers of another kind—often the same kind—take pleasure in cruel portraits of Jews by Richard Elman and Philip Roth.

Where injustice governs—where those who might reason have no faith in fair-mindedness or intelligence—propaganda replaces thought and art becomes impossible. Not that propaganda is the only route available to people intellectually debilitated by lack of love. If some people rant along party lines, others mournfully "tell it like it is," which normally means taking no position, simply copying down "reality" and throwing up one's hands. We have touched already on some of the causes of this.

If we are unable to distinguish between true morality—life-affirming, just, and compassionate behavior—and statistics (the all but hopeless situation of most of humanity) or, worse, trivial moral fashion, we begin to doubt morality itself. It becomes possible for a man as intelligent as Norman Mailer to speak of the murderer Charles Manson as "intellectually courageous," for the brave pursuit of truth changes utterly when truth becomes whim. The man so infected may begin to feel guilt chiefly for possessing a moral code at all. Confusion and doubt become the primary civilized emotions.

In such a society, as we've seen, the careless thinker can slide into the persuasion that the celebration of true morality has ceased to be the serious writer's function and may even be pernicious. If the writer, so persuaded, is a decent human being, he or she tends to adopt one of two humane and praiseworthy, but in the long run unfruitful, programs: either the writer celebrates important but passing concerns, such as social justice for particular minorities (dated and thus trivial once the goal has been achieved), or the writer serves only as historian, holding up the mirror to his age but not changing it, simply imitating, as Pound said, "its accelerated grimace." Both programs have, as I've said, their significance and value. I cannot believe that a true artist, living in America at the present time, can help involving himself in both, as well as in human errors less obvious. To fail to be concerned about social justice at a time when, even in the arena of international politics, the civilized impulse is involved with it as never before, would be a mark of artistic—almost criminal—frigidity, such limited perception as to make that person no writer at all. And to fail to imitate people as they are, even in a fable which takes as its setting ancient Nubia or outer space, would reveal a lack of the true artist's most noticeable characteristic: fascination with the feelings, gestures, obsessions, and phobias of the people of his own time and place. One cannot imagine a Dante, a Chaucer, a Shakespeare, or a Racine without characters drawn from a scrutiny of real people.

But in comparison with the true artist's celebration of the permanently moral, both programs are nevertheless secondary and can only produce art which, with the passing of its age, must lose force. Moreover, weak programs can lead to screeching, or straining for effect. E. L. Doctorow, in *Ragtime*, urges social justice in a more or less moving and persuasive way, but he is not concerned with true morality. After talk of policemen, evil capitalists, and strikebreakers, he has a scene in which the anarchist Emma Goldman gives a massage and a message to the now naked famous beauty Evelyn Nesbit, while a character known only as Mother's Younger Brother peeks from a closet. It's a scene filled, naturally, with prurient interest—there is nothing essentially wrong with that, from the point of view of the moral critic—and filled, also, with a strong and convincing tirade on women's rights. Though the relationship between the two women is not sexual, Evelyn is sexually aroused. Doctorow writes, dramatically ending his chapter:

Her pelvis rose from the bed as if seeking something in the air. Goldman was now at the bureau, capping her bottled emollient, her back to Evelyn as the younger woman began to ripple on the bed like a wave of the sea. At this moment a hoarse unearthly cry issued from the walls, the closet door flew open and Mother's Younger Brother fell into the room, his face twisted in a paroxysm of saintly mortification. He was clutching in his hands, as if trying to choke it, a rampant penis which, scornful of his intentions, whipped him about the floor, launching to his cries of ecstacy or despair, great filamented spurts of jism that traced the air like bullets and then settled slowly over Evelyn in her bed like falling ticker tape.

Reading Doctorow, Tolstoy would object, as he objected to Maupassant, that

lacking the first and perhaps the chief condition of good artistic production, a correct moral relation to what he described—that is to say, a knowledge of the difference between good and evil—he loved and described things that should not have been loved and described . . . he even describes certain obscenities difficult to understand.[11]

Tolstoy would of course be right; but the falsity of this passage runs much deeper. Though he can speak feelingly of women's rights, taking a stand that is moral, Doctorow's writing is meretricious, or at the very least frigid in Longinus' sense: the writer is not deeply involved in his characters' lives. Things do not happen in the world as Doctorow claims they do. Even in the hands of young and highly excited men, penises do not behave as Doctorow maintains. Doctorow's mind is elsewhere. He's after a flashy chapter ending, and reality can go knit. Bullets and ticker tape fall over poor victimized Evelyn, a matter we're intended to register as lightheartedly symbolic, teaching us a truth; but what truth the writer might have discovered if he'd carefully followed how things really do happen we will never know. The chicanery may even undermine the lesson he means to preach. Put off by fraudulence, the reader may incline to be suspicious of all the writer says, including what he says about women.

Among suivants of the second program, that of holding up a mirror to the age, the best is perhaps Donald Barthelme. He has a sharp eye for modern man's doubts and anxieties, free-floating guilt, politics, manners, turns of speech. In much of his fiction he aims at simple imitation in the form of comic-expressionistic cartoon. At times (as in "The Explanation"), he seems to aim at a certain kind of satire, but it's the satire of despair, not grounded on theory, implied in the work, of what ought to be, but constructed out of bemused weariness, irascibility, New York stylishness, and, sometimes, disgust. Both in drawings and in fictions, he imitates cleverly the modern world's sadness and confused sense of fear and loss, and in even the most fabulous or refracted of his fictions he keeps a careful eye on how the world really works. He has all the qualities of "talent" which Tolstoy listed in his early "Introduction to the Works of Guy de Maupassant," namely,

(1) a correct, that is, a moral relation of the author to his subject; (2) clearness of expression, or beauty of form—the two are identical; and (3) sincerity, that is, a sincere feeling of love or hatred of what the artist depicts.[12]

But in Barthelme all three qualities are enfeebled. He knows what is wrong, but he has no clear image of, or interest in, how things ought to be. Often, as in "Paraguay," he simply steps out of reality to play with the literary conventions which once helped us learn about the real. His form is elegant, but it suggests no beauty beyond literary shape, as if workmanship were now enough, there being no real value for that workmanship to struggle toward (only death for it to struggle against). And his sincerity is, though authentic, remote: he cares not about people but about ideas or "constructs"—in effect, painterly images: the Phantom of the Opera, Snow White more or less realistically conceived (neurotic modern life played against myth). His diagnosis of the evils of the age can be amusing, and perhaps, for some readers, moving. On occasion he celebrates a real human value, such as stubbornness, or touches on our tragic vulnerability, as in "Sentence." The world would be a duller place without him, as it would be without F. A. O. Schwartz. But no one would accuse him of creating what Tolstoy called "religious art." His world is not one of important values but only of values mislaid, emotions comically or sadly unrealized, a burden of mysteries no one has the energy to solve. It is a world he seems to have little wish to escape; or if one of his characters feels an urge to transcend the limitations of his world, as in "City of

Churches," we get only the resolve and promise, seldom the act. His writing has emotional control, clarity of style, and at least an impression of life's tragic waste; but even at his best, as in *The Dead Father*, Barthelme goes not for the profound but for the clever.

The limitation evident in a writer like Barthelme—and many lyric poets—is not moral shallowness, as it may first seem, but a species of Romantic self-love. Though I have said that he holds up a mirror to his age, Barthelme's effectiveness as a writer of fiction does not lie—as did the power of Tolstoy or Henry James—in seeing into other people's minds, even people the writer dislikes, and recreating diverse lives on paper, giving each character his moment of dignity and thus helping us to understand intellectually and intuitively both others and ourselves. Barthelme reflects his doubting and anxious age because he is, himself, an extreme representative of it. In this as in everything, it is worth noticing, he is a typical minor Romantic. Whereas for Montaigne or Wordsworth meditation on the self aims toward knowledge of humanity in general, and whereas for Pascal the self is hateful, getting in the way of communion with God, the minor Romantic is an egoist. At best he claims that, miserable as he may be, he's a model for imitation: better to be disillusioned than deluded. At worst he claims, as Rousseau did in his *Confessions*, "I am not like any one of those I've seen; I dare say I am unlike any man that exists." The modern Narcissus dreams up no large goals for all humanity because he's chiefly interested in his own kinks, pathetic or otherwise; and ironically, what a careful study of freaks reveals is that they're all alike. As we recognize our own moments of despair in the unmitigated gloom of Beckett, we recognize in all sad and weary writers common elements of ourselves, mainly our weakness. Romantic individualism should in the end make one fight for Greek freedom. There can be no truly moral art that isn't social, at least by implication (a point T. S. Eliot tried to deny in his essays but was driven to accept); and on the other hand, there can be no moral social art (as Doctorow's errors show) without honesty in the individual—the artist—as a premise for just and reasonable discussion.

Moral art in its highest form holds up models of virtue, whether they be heroic models like Homer's Achilles or models of quiet endurance, like the coal miners, the steelworkers, the Southern midwife, or the soldiers in the photographs of W. Eugene Smith. The artist so debilitated by guilt and self-doubt that he cannot be certain real virtues exist is an artist doomed to second-rate art, an artist of whom the best that can be said is that he's better, at least, than the consciously nihilistic artist or (worse, perhaps) the artist who believes in morality but has got it all wrong, so that he holds up for emulation what ought to be despised.

I mentioned earlier three causes of debilitating guilt in the modern world: the determinism of Freud, which undermines values by reading them as evasions, missing the self-evident fact that joy (not mere adjustment or satisfaction of hungers) is a chemical condition or psychological state actively sought and prized by human beings; the pessimism of Sartre, which undermines values by defining the future as a more or less fierce rejection of the present, a view which misses the fact that planning for the future is often a joyful affirmation of the present; and the logical and linguistic cautiousness of Wittgenstein, which, misunderstood, claims that truth does not exist—instead of saying, as Wittgenstein did, that certain forms of truth which do exist are philosophically inexpressible. And I have said that to be tricked by these false occasions of guilt is inevitably to limit one's art, abandoning eternal verities either for temporary and passing values or for empty imitation, without moral comment, of whatever conditions happen at the moment to exist.

This is not to condemn artistic representations in which the main point or feeling is simply the artist's compassion or love, as in Borges' *Minotaur,* the drab and mournful sculptures of George Segal, Shostakovich's musical laments for murdered Jews, or the photographs of André Kertész or Roman Visniac. A central feature in all these artists' work is the affirmation of universal human community or, as photographers say, "concern." Even Diane Arbus' fascination with the grotesque implies this affirmation, though what we mainly get in her work is her exaggerated sense of a universe gone wrong; we get from her, that is, a forced message of helplessness and despair. According to other photographers, Arbus' attempts to do straight commercial photography—for instance, photographs for record or book jackets—were regularly vitiated by her tendency to wait for the grimace. Neurotic concern, though it has interest, never has the power of concern in which all of us share.

For great art, even concern is not enough. Great art celebrates life's potential, offering a vision unmistakably and unsentimentally rooted in love. "Love" is of course another of those embarrassing words, perhaps a word even more embarrassing than "morality," but it's a word no aesthetician ought carelessly to drop from his vocabulary. Misused as it may be by pornographers and the makers of greeting-cards, it has, nonetheless, a firm, hard-headed sense that names the single quality without which true art cannot exist. It is a quality that shouts from the sculptures of Thomas Mallory, the music of Benjamin Britten and, among younger composers, Joseph Baber, and from good novels both slight and monumental—from John Irving or Toni Morrison

83

to Italo Calvino or Thomas Mann. Without love we get the ice-cold intellectual style of most academics or the worst fiction in *The New Yorker*.

Despite the labors of academic artists and those sophisticates who are embarrassed by emotion, it seems all but self-evident that it is for the pleasure of exercising our capacity to love that we pick up a book at all. Except in the classroom, where we read what is assigned, or study compositions or paintings to pass a course, we read or listen to or look at works of art in the hope of experiencing our highest, most selfless emotion, either to reach a sublime communication with the maker of the work, sharing his affirmations as common lovers do, or to find, in works of literature, characters we love as we do real people. Ultimately, in fact, plot exists only to give the characters means of finding and revealing themselves, and setting only to give them a place to stand. As for "thought," the element so quickly dismissed by Aristotle, it is simply what the characters say or would say if they were wiser and had our distance from their story. In art, morality and love are inextricably bound: we affirm what is good—for the characters in particular and for humanity in general—because we care. The artist who has no strong feeling about his characters—the artist who can feel passionate only about his words or ideas—has no urgent reason to think hard about the characters' problems, the "themes" in his fiction. He imitates human gesture in the movements of his puppets, but he does not worry as a father worries about the behavior of his son; and the result is a fictional universe one would not want one's loved ones forced to inhabit.

This is the final point John Fowles makes in his novel on the modern novel, *Daniel Martin*: "*No true compassion without will, no true will without compassion.*" Without will—the artist's conscious determination to take his characters and their problems seriously—no artist can achieve real compassion. And without compassion—without real and deep love for his "subjects" (the people he writes about and, by extension, all human beings)—no artist can summon the will to make true art; he will be satisfied, instead, with clever language or with cynical jokes and too easy, dire solutions like those common in contemporary fiction.

At the risk of belaboring Fowles' point, briefly consider what happens in the work of three contemporary American novelists who have been widely praised: Norman Mailer, Kurt Vonnegut, Jr., and Joseph Heller. None of the three cares enough about his characters to use them as anything but examples in a forced proof. The novelist's "message," in each case, is only loosely related to the characters: they exist for the sake of the predetermined message, not as subjects for the artist's open-minded exploration of what he can honestly say.

Think of Mailer's *Why Are We In Vietnam?* Mailer's central character, haunted by his black "brother," is less a lifelike human being than a convenience by means of which the writer can bring forward his racial myth, that American feelings about Vietnam grew out of our feelings about our brother blacks, so that all that was important about that war lay within us. Since we get no real analysis of character, we must take the myth—or else deny it—as dogma; and even if we happen to be persuaded by the myth, so that we believe with Mailer that some sort of Vietnam was inevitable, it leaves us unsatisfied as an answer to the title question; the myth treats as irrelevant all the more obvious causes of the war—the feeling of some Americans that we were holding to a commitment, the Pentagon's wish to keep the resources of southern Asia out of Chinese hands, and so forth. When the novelist's imaginary world is too carelessly constructed to test conditions in the real world, even the novelist's ideas suffer.

An American Dream is similarly damaged by Mailer's greater interest in his ideas than in his characters, and here too Mailer's lack of concern about people wrecks his effort to think out ideas. The opening chapter of *An American Dream* presents an exact and compelling description of a state that comes over all of us on occasion, a state of entrancement—well understood by tightrope artists and motorcycle racers—wherein everything we do seems perfectly in tune with the universe, unthinkingly right. The observation from life is worthy of serious novelistic exploration, but Mailer, whether from laziness or from preacherly arrogance—an assumption that he knows all the answers in advance—settles for easy satire, and, worse yet, satire of an American set of attitudes that, because he so largely shares them, he cannot convincingly spoof. The result is a half-satirical, half-boyishly-earnest novel about Americans and witchcraft.

What Mailer's imagination gives him is almost always better than what he can find to do with it. Think of the power in that nightmare image, from the same novel, of the narrator's phone call to the dead Marilyn Monroe. Literally and symbolically, the moment is superb: according to the usual stereotype, at least, Americans do have a dream of perfection, a violent wish to break down even the barriers of death to reach the True, Good, and Beautiful—ideal forms for which, in our infantilism, we can think of no higher expression than a pitifully dead movie star-calendar girl. The impossible phone call can make the hair on the back of our necks rise, but Mailer's hero is unworthy of the symbol, a stick-figure bully not even Mailer likes, a creature halfheartedly created for a halfhearted satire.

Vonnegut and Heller are similarly inventive and similarly cool-hearted, in their differing ways, about their characters. Vonnegut's writing is a classic example of what Fowles means when he speaks of inadequate will. Vonnegut reportedly has a theory that one should say no more than necessary, so that description consists of, in effect, one-liners, and character is tone, mostly the same tone throughout. The result is that his novels have the feel of first-class comic books (trash culture elevated to art, if you will) and can easily be read by people who dislike long sentences. Possibly Vonnegut is not telling the whole story when he speaks of his theory of keeping things short. He also tells us that he endlessly rewrites, and though that's surprising, since revision often leads to subtlety and richness, Vonnegut is doubtless telling the truth. If so, then his problem as an artist may be partly psychological: he's overcritical of himself, endlessly censoring, endlessly reconsidering his moral affirmations. That would explain the seeming cold-heartedness and trivial-mindedness of his famous comment on the American fire-bombing of Dresden, "So it goes," a desperate, perhaps overcensored attitude mindlessly echoed by the turned-off and cynical. Vonnegut's cynical disciples read him wrong, of course. It is Vonnegut himself who points out the vast and systematic modern evils that he then appears to shrug off or, for some reason, blame on God. But the misreading is natural. Vonnegut's moral energy is forever flagging, his fight forever turning slapstick. He's most himself when, as in *Breakfast of Champions* or his *Saturday Evening Post* stories, he's most openly warmhearted and comic. His lack of commitment—ultimately a lack of concern about his characters—makes his writing slight.

While Vonnegut sighs, grins, and sidles away, Heller grinds on and on, painstakingly mirroring his age without escaping or defining it. For all its popularity a few years ago, we need not say anything now about *Catch-22*. It was in its moment interesting and amusing, but it reads now like old news, still funny in many places but remote, nostalgically curious. *Something Happened* is a more important book, a work with a large measure of authentic feeling and insight, but one that will last no longer than *Catch-22*, chiefly because no one, not even Heller, can stand Bob Slocum, the central character.

Nothing happens in *Something Happened*. A change occurs in Slocum—the same change that has recently occurred in America as a whole, from passivity, hopelessness, and helplessness to action, cautious optimism, and the beginnings of responsibility. But the change is groundless and sinister, Heller tells us. It is a change that comes out of climate, not conscious moral choice. The narrator describes, early in the novel, his general feeling of futility. He thinks of his check, on which is printed the warning that "checks must not be spindled, torn, defaced, stapled, or mutilated in any other way." Bob Slocum muses:

What would happen, I speculate gloomily every two weeks or so as I tear open the blank, buff pay envelope and stare dully at the holes and numbers and words on my punch-card paycheck as though hoping disappointedly for some large, unrectifiable mistake in my favor, if I did spindle, fold, tear, deface, staple, and mutilate it? (It's my paycheck, isn't it? Or is it?) What would happen if, deliberately, calmly, with malice aforethought and obvious premeditation, I disobeyed?

I know what would happen: Nothing would happen. And the knowledge depresses me. Some girl downstairs I never saw before (probably with bad skin also) would simply touch a few keys on some kind of steel key punch that would set things right again, and it would be as though I had not disobeyed at all. My act of rebellion would be absorbed like rain on an ocean and leave no trace. I would not cause a ripple.

That helplessness, that feeling of imprisonment in meaningless, dull system, was a common state of mind in the late sixties and early seventies, when Heller was working on this book. Even for many noble, life-affirming people there seemed no way out but miracle, some such terrible miracle as happens in Heller's novel, releasing Bob Slocum from his own weakness and at least one of his painful psychological burdens, the existence of his loving, pitiful idiot son:

> "Something happened!" a youth in his early teens calls excitedly to a friend and goes running ahead to look.
>
> A crowd is collecting at the shopping center. A car has gone out of control and mounted the sidewalk. A plate glass window has been smashed. My boy is lying on the ground. (He has not been decapitated.) He is screaming in agony and horror, with legs and arms twisted brokenly and streams of blood spurting from holes in his face and head and pouring down over one hand from inside a sleeve. He spies me with a start and extends an arm. He is panic-stricken. So am I.
>
> "Daddy!"
>
> He is dying. A terror, a pallid, pathetic shock more dreadful than any I have ever been able to imagine, has leaped into his face. I can't stand it. He can't stand it. He hugs me. He looks beggingly at me for help. His screams are piercing. I can't bear to see him suffering such agony and fright. I have to do something. I hug his face deeper into the crook of my shoulder. I hug him tightly with both my arms. I squeeze.
>
> "Death," says the doctor, "was due to asphyxiation. The boy was smothered."

Despite Heller's novelistic power, *Something Happened* is finally not profound but only sad-sardonic and thus unsatisfying. Like Vonnegut, Heller refuses to take any bold, potentially embarrassing moral stand. People like Slocum aren't worth it to him. It is true that *Something Happened* is no mere entertainment but life's raw material thoughtfully digested, thoroughly made "real" as a dream in the reader's mind. But the fictive dream is merely a fable on our troubles; it is never transformed into healing vision or affirmation. Whereas Vonnegut avoids commitment with a boyish grin and a shrug, Heller mockingly imitates the Satanist's leer. Slocum does not fight or think his way to freedom and responsibility; he is, literally, possessed by it—demonically possessed. At the start of the novel he was unable to act, filled with real and neurotic fears. At the end, pushed by chance into facing his nightmare, even killing his son, he finds himself—strangely—in a position of control. As the novel closes, a typist, Martha, whom Slocum has for months recognized as drifting toward madness, crushed by the office's cold, inhuman system, finally snaps. Slocum handles the situation "like a ballet master." Everything goes right for him, as for Mailer's witches in *An American Dream*, and Slocum gets the madwoman out of there. But all is not well. Mad Martha is exactly like Slocum. As he wept after killing his child and made the people around him solicitous, and as he learned to dominate "a much higher class of executive," so it is, Slocum sees, with the madwoman as she "rises compliantly, smiling, with a hint of *diabolical satisfaction* . . . at the wary attention she has succeeded in extorting from so many people who are solicitous and alarmed." (My italics.) The novel's closing line is thus grimly ironic: "Everyone seems pleased with the way I've taken command." The dark twist is dramatically interesting and may be said to make a point: indifferent system makes devils of us all. Certainly Heller's novel is vastly superior to *The Exorcist* or, worse, *The Omen* and *Rosemary's Baby*; but Heller does not care enough to search out an answer to the real question: What are we to do?

Though their methods differ, all three of the writers I've been discussing are essentially transcribers of the moods of their time. They do not really think things out, though unlike post-modernists they to some extent claim to be truth-tellers. Focusing on "message" and indifferent to real human beings, as represented by their characters, they take either no position or else smug, slogany positions. In place of wisdom and careful analysis, products of the artist's will and compassion, they offer, if anything, cant, cynicism, or dramatic gimmickry—interesting and arresting infernal entertainment, but nothing that will hold, nothing that will help.

We find a subtler kind of failure in the most admired of the old-fashioned moderns, Saul Bellow, actually not a novelist at heart but an essayist disguised as a writer of fiction. In *Seize the Day*, *Augie March*, and *Henderson the Rain King*, Bellow makes serious use of fictional techniques, but even there the essayist-lecturer is always ready to step in, stealing the stage from the fictional characters to make the fiction more "important." The morality of art is, as I've said, far less a matter of doctrine than of process. Art is the means by which an artist comes to see; it is his peculiar, highly sophisticated and extremely demanding technique of discovery. Hence the artist—even the essentially great artist—who indulges himself, treating his art as a plaything, a mere vehicle for his ego and abstract ideas, is like a man who uses his spectacles to swat flies.

Bellow's self-indulgence takes various forms. On occasion it appears as stylistic fiddling—as language designed mainly to show off Bellow's gifts as philosopher, poet, mimic, or Jewish humorist—not aimed, as it should be, at clarifying action and character or at controlling the reader's attention and response, heightening his pleasure and understanding. When Bellow is feeling self-indulgent, his language, instead of sharpening effects, distracts the reader, calls attention to the writer and thus away from the story unfolding like a dream in the reader's mind. And he frequently makes other, more serious mistakes. Chiefly, he allows himself—or the single character who dominates each novel—too much talk. Fiction goes after understanding by capturing, through imitation, "the ineluctable modality of the world"—that is, characters who subtly embody values and who test them, with clear but inexpressible results, in action. Discursive thought is not fiction's most efficient tool; the interaction of characters is everything. But Bellow can almost never handle more than one character at a time (an exception, perhaps, is his creation of both Humboldt and Citrine in *Humboldt's Gift*), and that one major character, Bellow's surrogate, has always an inordinate love of talk. At every opportunity, Bellow leans his characters and action on some door frame, turns off his fiction's clock, and, from behind the mask of his hero, expatiates. When the essay voice begins, we are asked to appreciate, mainly on the basis of the speaker's charm, a set of prejudices and opinions, or shrewd observations—it makes no great difference—that have nothing to do, directly, with the progress of the action or the values under test. This is not to deny that characters ought to ruminate, if it suits them, from time to time. (Tolstoy is the proof.) It's a question of degree—at some point enough is enough—and a question of artistic illusion—a Republican reader should not be personally offended by some character's unfair attack on Eisenhower. We allow characters to be themselves; we delight in their foolishness; but if the reader knows in his bones that the attack is Bellow's own, that Bellow cares more about his political opinion than he does about maintaining the artistic illusion of a coherent, self-sustained fictional world, then the reader has good reason for throwing out the book. In Bellow such slips of the mask are common—as they are in late Tolstoy or, as Virginia Woolf pointed out, in Charlotte Bronte.

Bellow may sometimes get away with his intrusions, partly because of his comic gift and his gift for finding powerful symbols—for instance the symbol of the moral individual buried alive in *Mr. Sammler's Planet*—and also because his opinions often strike the reader as carefully thought out and wise. Certainly his stand is boldly opposed to those trashy popular philosophies we so often encounter in other writers' work—cynical nihilism or the winking, mugging despair of Thomas Pynchon (Bellow counters with a theory of faith and responsible love); self-regarding existentialism (Bellow offers, instead, a theory of universal relatedness in which animals and people have certain common woes); tyrannical Marxism and a whining hatred of "American business" (Bellow offers, instead, a view of people—even naive communists and crass business people—as individuals, of suffering as universal and a thing to be dealt with, and of history as a moral search). And it is true, too, that though Bellow's intrusions offend, they nevertheless prove that Bellow can still feel unabashed concern. But the fact remains that Bellow's novels come off in the end as sprawling works of advice, not art.

The generous critic might hold up numerous other writers as important artists—John Barth, Thomas Pynchon, Joyce Carol Oates, Robert Coover, Donald Barthelme, James Purdy, William Gaddis, John Hawkes, Katherine Anne Porter, Guy Davenport, John Cheever, Bernard Malamud, J. D. Salinger, Eudora Welty, and John Updike, to name a few. How many of them will outlast the century? Perhaps Malamud, certainly a powerful artist at his best; conceivably Guy Davenport, if sheer precision and uncompromising artistry count, but his output is spare and his work goes underadvertized; possibly Eudora Welty, because of one superb novel, *Losing Battles*, a handful of stories, and her secure position as Southerner and woman in our college American literature courses; possibly Joyce Carol Oates, for a few excellent short stories; possibly Salinger. But I suspect that what I've typed above is a list of inflated reputations. Some on the list will die quickly, of pure meanness—Porter, Coover, and Gaddis—and some will die of intellectual blight, academic narrowness, or fakery—Pynchon, Updike (or most of his work), and Barth.

Barth, as the most mentioned of all "innovative fictionists," as he likes to say, is the most interesting case. His first two novels, *The Floating Opera* and *The End of the Road* (one must read the 1967 edition, not the editorially altered and morally preferable 1958 edition), are his most controlled and conventional. Both have a novel, academic sort of charm, for instance the hokey but not overblown symbolism of life as an opera passing down the river, so that no one on shore can get the plot; both have a rare vividness of imagery and dramatization and a strong sense of place; and both have wonderful comic moments carefully drawn from life. But both are weakened to the point of collapse by vulgarities of style and by opinions that will not survive scrutiny, chiefly the "elitist" notion, as Fowles says, that life is absurd, a notion implying that justifications for human actions must be imposed upon, not discovered within, human nature. And both have that troublesome defect we find in nearly all Barth's fiction, the touch of life-hate which reveals itself in the author's fascination with the ugly, the disgusting. Where it comes from one cannot make out, since in other respects Barth seems all sunshine and good cheer—even his nihilism, as he says himself, is "cheerful."

Barth's later books are more ambitious and fake. For all the praise afforded it, the antique language of *The*

Sot-Weed Factor is an aesthetic miscalculation. If we finish the novel, and for all its linguistic cuteness *The Sot-Weed Factor* is worth finishing, we do so largely despite the language and despite those weighty passages where Barth labors embarrassingly after "meaning." We read the book for its humor, Barth's innocent, high-spirited pleasure in the eighteenth-century kind of novel he's imitating, and perhaps to some extent for Barth's wide-eyed delight in ideas we've heard before. We read the book, in other words, because Barth's mostly sunny personality comes through, and to sunny people we are willing to allow almost anything.

Giles Goat-Boy pushed human tolerance further. Despite some dazzling plays of wit (not always a good thing), the book is all but unreadable—arch, extravagantly self-indulgent, clumsily allegorical, pedantic, tiresomely and pretentiously advance guard, and like much of our "new fiction" puerilely obscene. *Chimera* has many of the same faults but at least is shorter, and here, more than in the earlier books, Barth comes through as a loving, optimistic man. We meet here, despite the centrality of the love theme, Barth's usual rather curious underestimation of women, his usual partly charming, partly tiresome egoism (he speaks of one of his own ideas for a piece of fiction as "inspired"), more allegorical string-pulling, and a curious oscillation between fascination with the cruel and ugly, on the one hand, and, on the other, an inclination toward mush. What will the future think, we sigh, of all that flippancy—Scheherazade as "Sherry," Duniazade as "Dooney"? Again and again we remark with John Gay, "This miserable scene demands a groan."

An odd thing about Barth is that he always seems to know what's wrong with his fiction but never fixes it. In his short piece "Life Story" he has his fictional writer muse, while working on his tiresomely Barthian story,

Another story about a writer writing a story! Another *regressus in in-finitum!* Who doesn't prefer art that at least overtly imitates some-thing other than its own processes? That doesn't continually pro-claim "Don't forget I'm an artifice!"? That takes for granted its mimetic nature instead of asserting it in order (not so slyly after all) to deny it, or vice-versa? Though his critics sympathetic and other-wise described his own work as avant-garde, in his heart of hearts he disliked literature of an experimental, self-despising, or overtly metaphysical character, like Samuel Beckett's, Marian Cutler's, Jorge Borges's. The logical fantasies of Lewis Carroll pleased him less than straight-forward tales of adventure, subtly sentimental romances, even densely circumstantial realisms like Tolstoy's. . . .

The fictional writer and the actual John Barth at the top of the regressus continue the story in spite of all this because, boring as the story may be, both actually and theoretically, the metaphysical and aesthetic questions involved in its boringness are, to Barth, interesting. Similarly, when a character in *Chimera* comments on Barth's self-conscious style, the character John Barth ac-knowledges the fault but lets it stand. So in "Lost in the Fun-house," one of his best pieces of fiction, Barth speaks shrewdly of the problem of the artist who gets so lost in his gimmickry that he forgets the human pur-poses it has been invented to serve; yet in all his fiction Barth is tangled helplessly in his own wiring.

What are we to say of the writer who admits his faults and clings to them? We may praise him for self-knowledge (self-knowledge is easier than many people think), praise him for frankness (a goose hissing at you in the yard is being frank), or we may, with polite apol-ogies, throw away the book because self-knowledge and that sort of frankness are not what we came for. Barth can tell stories, but most of the time he doesn't, preferring artistic self-consciousness.

As Fowles has shown in all his fiction, self-con-sciousness need not be a fault. All art is studied. But it is one thing to struggle by laborious art for the voice of straightforward, sober-minded thought, the voice that announces in no uncertain terms that the enterprise is serious even when amusing (as in Fielding's *Tom Jones*), the entirely trustworthy, authoritative voice that leads us through *Pride and Prejudice*, or *The Sleepwalkers*, or *The Golden Bowl*. (The voice may sometimes be ironic, even as blackly ironic as the voices in *The Confidence Man;* or it may speak in dialect, like Huck Finn. Conviction is what counts.) It's one thing, in short, to achieve by craft and extravagant trickery—by that frantic sort of posturing through which bad men learn goodness in the *Nichomachian Ethics*—a totally authentic, reliable narrator like Daniel Martin. It's another thing entirely to achieve by tortuous industry the empty novelty of the writer whose main concern seems to be with remaining advance guard.

The difference between what merits being called classical prose and the prose of most of our writers is a matter of confidence, of belief. Our more fashionable writers feel, as Chekhov and Tolstoy did not, that their art is unimportant; and they're correct. I have already mentioned one exception, John Fowles. Perhaps there are others. John Cheever's "singing voice," as he puts it—in both the short stories and in the novels, and in both works which use old-fashioned realism, as in the Wapshot books, and in books more innovative, *Bullet Park* and *Falconer*—is clear and sure; but he's careless about other things—for instance, about authenticating fictional facts such as, in *Falconer*, Ferrigut's taking of methadone and his murder of his brother. Despite these slips and others, Cheever's writing has importance: since he cares about his characters and cares about the reader, his affirmations are sufficiently hard-won to stand up. He qualifies his optimistic Christian vision with the necessary measure of irony (for instance, at the end of *Bullet Park*, where Nailles, after saving his son's life, is not much better than before); and though he asserts, like any good Christian, that miracles occur, he does not ask us or his characters to count on them. Malamud's affirmations also stand up, and though his novels sometimes sprawl, his control of the emotional material, rooted in concern about his characters' lives, is as sure as Cheever's.

The same cannot be said, it seems to me, of John Updike. He's a master of symbolic complexity, but one can't tell his women apart in a book like *Couples;* his characters' sexual preoccupations, mostly perverse, are too generously indulged; and the disparity between the surface and sub-surface of his novels is treacherous: to the naive reader (and most readers of popular best sellers are likely to be naive), a novel like *A Month of Sundays* seems a merry, bourgeois-pornographic book about a minister who likes copulation, while to the subtler reader, the novel may be wearily if not ambivalently satirical, a sophisticated attack on false religion. (As Jesus went into the wilderness to be tested, Updike's minister-hero goes into the desert, sent by his church, in order to come to grips with his promiscuity problem. There he seduces his keeper, symbolically identified with God.) Since the irony—the presumably satiric purpose—is nowhere available on the surface, since the novel can easily be read as a piece of neo-orthodox Presbyterian heresy (Christ has redeemed us in advance, so let's fornicate), one cannot help feeling misgivings about Updike's intent. Certainly he appeals, intentionally or not, to the two chief heart-warmers of the mindless in America, religion and sex. Protestant Christianity has always contained one great risk, a risk against which the best Christians always keep guard: like Marxism, it has a tendency to make light of reason and individual tragedy (God will provide, and heaven cancels death). Like Rabbit, in *Rabbit,*

Run, who dislikes contraceptives and takes no thought of the harm his attentions may do to women, the optimistic Christian may be inclined to leave too much to heaven. John Updike worries no more about his characters and his readers than does Rabbit about his women.

Even if, for all my doubts, Updike's moral intent is unmistakable—even if a Buddhist or Muslim is sure to notice that Rabbit's problem is pursuit of empty ritual—we feel another worry, I think. The novels, properly understood, may be too much like sermons. No man can serve two masters, the artistic ideal, which makes its premise an essential and radical openness to persuasion, and the religious ideal, which, like Nietzsche's superman, is "deaf to even the best counterarguments." Whether one looks at low-brow religious artists or at sophisticated highbrows like John Updike or, better, Frederick Buechner, one discovers pretty quickly Who's paying them. Religion's chief value is its conservatism: it keeps us in touch with what at least one section of humanity has believed for centuries. Art's chief value is that it takes nothing for granted. The novels of Buechner, an ordained minister, show no signs of an attempt to disguise their intent, which is why, as we read Buechner, we trust him. Knowing where he stands, Buechner can explore, dramatically and openly, the conflicts in his religion, and though we can guess in advance that his solutions will be orthodox, we admire the honesty with which he seeks out a personal understanding of the orthodox answers. Updike's subtler method inspiries no such trust, though his conclusions seem equally determined. Bernard Malamud has said that great writing leads constantly into surprises, and that the writer should be the first one surprised. Unlike Buechner's—since Buechner lays his cards on the table, at least as far as message is concerned, surprising us only with character revelations—Updike's surprises, once we've figured out the symbols, are the theological conclusions we should have expected. Yet for all these reservations—and the further reservation that Updike's humor seems to me not funny—I must admit that on a few occasions, especially in *The Centaur,* he proves himself an artist.

But granting the exceptions—Bellow, Malamud, on rare occasions Updike, and no doubt various others—the fact remains that our serious fiction is quite bad. The emphasis, among younger artists, on surface and novelty of effect is merely symptomatic. The sickness goes deeper, to an almost total loss of faith in—or perhaps understanding of—how true art works. True art, by specific technical means now commonly forgotten, clarifies life, establishes models of human action, casts nets toward the future, carefully judges our right and wrong directions, celebrates and mourns. It does not rant. It does not sneer or giggle in the face of death, it invents prayers and weapons. It designs visions worth trying to make fact. It does not whimper or cower or throw up its hands and bat its lashes. It does not make hope contingent on acceptance of some religious theory. It strikes like lightning, or *is* lightning; whichever.

We need to stop excusing mediocre and downright pernicious art, stop "taking it for what it's worth" as we take our fast foods, our overpriced cars that are no good, the overpriced houses we spend all our lives fixing, our television programs, our schools thrown up like barricades in the way of young minds, our brainless fat religions, our poisonous air, our incredible cult of sports, and our ritual of fornicating with all pretty or even horse-faced strangers. We would not put up with a debauched king, but in a democracy all of us are kings, and we praise debauchery as pluralism. This book is of course no condemnation of pluralism; but it is true that art is in one sense fascistic: it claims, on good authority, that some things are healthy for individuals and society and some things are not. Unlike the fascist in uniform, the artist never forces anyone to anything. He merely makes his case, the strongest case possible. He lights up the darkness with a lightning flash, protects his friends the gods—that is, values—and all humanity without exception, and then moves on.

PART II

PRINCIPLES OF ART
AND CRITICISM

1

Moral Fiction

TO MAINTAIN that true art is moral one need not call up theory; one need only think of the fictions that have lasted: *The Iliad* and *The Odyssey;* the tragedies of Aeschylus, Sophocles, and Euripides; Virgil's *Aeneid;* Dante's *Commedia;* the plays of Shakespeare and Racine; the novels of Tolstoy, Melville, Thomas Mann, James Joyce. Such works—all true works of art—can exert their civilizing influence century after century, long after the cultures that produced them have decayed. Yet it is clearly not true that the morality of art takes care of itself, the good, like gravity, inevitably prevailing. Good art is always in competition with bad, and though the long-run odds for good art are high, since cultures that survive almost by definition take pleasure in the good, even the good in a foreign tongue, the short-term odds are discouraging. The glories of Greece and Rome are now bones on old hills. Civilized virtue, in states or individuals, can easily become too complex for self-defense, can be forced simply to abdicate like those few late Roman emperors not murdered on the street. And like a civilized Roman, the creator of good art—the civilized artist—can easily fall into a position of disadvantage, since he can recognize virtues in the kind of art he prefers not to make, can think up excuses and justifications for even the cheapest pornography—to say nothing of more formidable, more "serious" false art—while the maker of trash, the barbarian, is less careful to be just. It is a fact of life that noble ideas, noble examples of human behavior, can drop out of fashion though they remain as real and applicable as ever—can simply come to be forgotten, plowed under by "progress."

I would not claim that even the worst bad art should be outlawed, since morality by compulsion is a fool's morality and since, moreover, I agree with Tolstoy that the highest purpose of art is to make people good by choice. But I do think bad art should be revealed for what it is whenever it dares to stick its head up, and I think the arguments for the best kind of art should be mentioned from time to time, because our appreciation of the arts is not wholly instinctive. If it were, our stock of bad books, paintings, and compositions would be somewhat less abundant.

I have said that wherever possible moral art holds up models of decent behavior; for example, characters in fiction, drama, and film whose basic goodness and struggle against confusion, error, and evil—in themselves and in others—give firm intellectual and emotional support to our own struggle. Sometimes, admittedly, the essentially moral artist may ignore this end, limiting his art to a search for information; that is, imaginative capture of what could not be known otherwise. A brilliantly imagined novel about a rapist or murderer can be more enlightening than a thousand psycho-sociological studies; and implied praise or condemnation in such a novel may be irrelevant or petty-minded. Work of this kind has obvious value and may even be beautiful in its execution, but it is only in a marginal sense art. At other times the moral model may be indirect, as when the confusion of Chaucer's Pardoner or Shakespeare's Macbeth leaves true morality at least partly to implication or at best in the hands of some minor character. Indirect models are hardly to be despised; nonetheless, it should be noticed that life's imitation of art is direct and not necessarily intelligent. After Marlon Brando appeared in *On the Waterfront*, an entire generation took to slumping, mumbling, turning up its collar, and hanging its cigarette casually off the lip. After the appearance of Roy Rogers, hordes of twelve-year-olds took to squinting. Today, though perhaps not in Shakespeare's day, the resolution never to behave like Macbeth does not inevitably carry any clear implication of what to do instead.

For the person who looks at fiction mainly from the point of view of the reader or critic, it is easy to get the idea that fiction is serious, thoughtful, or "philosophical" merely because—and merely in the sense that—some writers of fiction are intelligent thinkers who express their profound ideas through stories. Thus Henry James tells us about American innocence, Melville shows us how the quality of life is affected by the proposition of an indifferent universe, and so on. What literary critics claim is true: writers do communicate ideas. What the writer understands, though the student or critic of literature need not, is that the writer discovers, works out, and tests his ideas in the process of writing. Thus at its best fiction is, as I've said, a way of thinking, a philosophical method.

It must be granted at once that some good and "serious" fiction is merely first-class propaganda—fiction in which the writer knows before he starts what it is that he means to say and does not allow his mind to be changed by the process of telling the story. A good deal of medieval literature works in this way. The doctrine is stock, and the actions of ladies, gentlemen, and beasts are merely devices for communicating doctrine in a pleasing way. This is the method Boccaccio describes in his *Genealogy of the Gods* as the essential technique of allegory; it produces the kind of poetry Sidney defends in his *Defense:* instruction clothed in delight. *Pilgrim's Progress* and *Gulliver's Travels* (to some extent) are fictions of this kind, as are (to a large extent) such modern works as *Gravity's Rainbow*. Fiction of this sort, dogmatic or ironic-dogmatic fiction, may be highly entertaining, may be fully persuasive, may have the clear ring of art; but such fiction is closer to the sermon than to the true short story or novel, closer to the verse essay as practiced by Pope than to the Elizabethan play. Such fiction may be—and usually is—*moralistic,* and the writer, in creating it, may be morally careful—that is, may work hard at telling nothing but the truth; but in what I am describing as true moral fiction, the "art" is not merely ornamental: it controls the argument and gives it its rigor, forces the writer to intense yet dispassionate and unprejudiced watchfulness, drives him—in ways abstract logic cannot match—to unexpected discoveries and, frequently, a change of mind.

Moral fiction communicates meanings discovered by the process of the fiction's creation. We can see the process working when we look through the drafts of a certain kind of writer's work. Thus we see Tolstoy beginning with one set of ideas and attitudes in *Two Marriages,* an early draft of *Anna Karenina*—in which Anna, incredible as it seems, marries Vronsky—and gradually discovering, draft by draft, deeper and deeper implications in his story, revising his judgments, stumbling upon connections, reaching new insights, until finally he nails down the attitudes and ideas we find dramatized, with such finality and conviction that it seems to us unthinkable that they should not have burst full-grown from Tolstoy's head, in the published novel. So Dostoevski agonized over the better and worse implications of Myshkin's innocence and impotence. We see the same when we look at successive drafts of work by Kafka, or even the two drafts of Chaucer's *Troilus and Criseyde*.

The writing of a fiction is *not* a mode of thought when a good character and a bad one are pitted against each other. There is nothing inherently wrong with such fiction. It may be funny, or biting, or thrillingly melodramatic; it may be unspeakably witty, or grave, or mysterious, or something else; but it can contain only cleverness and preachments, not the struggle of thought. When fiction becomes thought—a kind of thought less restricted than logic or mere common sense (but also impossible to verify)—the writer makes discoveries which, in the act of discovering them in his fiction, he communicates to the reader.

He makes these discoveries in several ways. Much of what a writer learns he learns simply by imitation. Making up a scene, he asks himself at every step, "Would she really say that?" or "Would he really throw the shoe?" He plays the scene through in his imagination, taking all the parts, being absolutely fair to everyone involved (mimicking each in turn, as Aristotle pointed out, and never sinking to stereotype for even the most minor characters), and when he finishes the scene he understands by sympathetic imitation what each character has done throughout and why the fight, or accident, or whatever, developed as it did. The writer does the same with the total action. Throughout the entire chain of causally related events, the writer asks himself, would *a* really cause *b* and not *c*, etc., and he creates what seems, at least by the test of his own imagination and experience of the world, an inevitable development of story. Inevitability does not depend, of course, on realism. Some or all of the characters may be fabulous—dragons, griffins, Achilles' talking horses—but once a character is established for a creature, the creature must act in accord with it.

To learn about reality by mimicking it, needless to say, the writer must never cheat. He may establish any sort of *givens* he pleases, but once they are established he must follow where, in his experience, nature would lead if there really were, say, griffins. He cannot, for instance, make the reader accept some event on the basis of the writer's stylistic eloquence. By rhetoric any writer worth his salt can convince the reader that an eighty-pound griffin falls twice as fast as a forty-pound griffin, but if natural law in a world containing griffins is one of the premises the writer has accepted, the rhetoric is a betrayal of honest thought. Neither can the honest writer make the reader accept what he says took place if the writer moves from a to b by verbal sleight of hand; that is, by distracting the reader. It is easy for any clever writer to evoke and fully authenticate a situation (a), then digress to something else, then evoke and fully authenticate a situation which pretends to be the direct effect of a, a situation b which is in fact implausible as a result of a but does not seem implausible because the digression has blurred the real and inevitable effect of a in the reader's mind. No decent writer, one might suppose, would play such games—except, by accident, on himself. Yet many contemporary writers do, and some, like Stanley Elkin, do it on principle, preferring comic surprise to energetic discovery and looking for fictive energy not in character and action but in the power of the writer's performance or in poetic language. It is true that the freedom to follow wherever language may lead can sometimes result in the ambush of unexpected insights; and it is true, too, that Stanley Elkin no more tells conscious lies in his fiction than did John Bunyan. Nevertheless, it requires a very special talent to succeed in Elkin's way, and one may wonder if the race is worth the candle. The writer who boasts, "I can make a lady pick up a coffee cup anytime I please" may be amusing, even spell-binding, like a circus performer, but he is not, in one of the available ways, serious. Worse, the strong likelihood is that his work will be, in one important way, boring.

It's because an arbitrary plot is likely to be boring in the end that Aristotle objected to a plot solution by divine machinery. If Aristotle's position were still generally understood, we would need to say no more on this subject; but unfortunately, in recent years Aristotle's ideas have fallen out of fashion among some modern writers, a group which includes, of course, Stanley Elkin and is in some measure lead by William Gass.

Gass claims—and conceivably for some readers it's true—that when a writer describes a scene, the reader's imagination seizes only those details the writer has explicitly given, so that, for example, if the writer mentions that a character wears spectacles but says nothing else about that character, the reader forms no impression of the character's nose, eyes, forehead, stature, or clothes. If it is true that words are the writer's only material, then the only kind of richness or interest available to the writer is linguistic, and—given equal linguistic dazzle—there should be no difference between the emotional effect of a story about a lifelike character with some urgent problem (Gass, of course, would disapprove of the word *lifelike*) and a character who insists that she has no existence except as words on a page. To think of a fictional character as a person—

to weep for little Nell or shudder at the effrontery of Captain Ahab—is, in this view, childishly naive.

The trouble with the theory is this: words have associations, and groups of words form chains of association. To say the word *crate* to a native English speaker is to summon up an image of a crate and, with it, the natural background of that image, which is a different background from that summoned up by *casque* or *trunk* or *cube*. To say that a character is built like a crate is to suggest far more than just the character's shape: it is to hint at his personality, his station in life, even his behavior. This becomes obvious when we place the character in some setting not at all natural for a crate and then linguistically reinforce the unnaturalness: *He sat at the tea table, fiddling with his spoon, as stiff and unnatural as a crate.* It is true that the metaphor established an "idea," an intellectual perception of the character, but a more important truth is that the idea has an inextricable emotional charge: depending on context we are sorry for the crate, amused by it, or annoyed. One of the essentials of our humanness (or animalness, perhaps) is that we empathize—it's our chief way of learning. And the more complex the pattern of ideational connections—that is, the more fully we understand the scene adding up facts, metaphors, and rhythms—the more completely we slip, unwittingly, *into* it, pitying, smiling at, or despising the crate. Thus the idea that the writer's only material is words is true only in a trivial sense. Words conjure emotionally charged images in the reader's mind, and when the words are put together in the proper way, with the proper rhythms— long and short sounds, smooth or ragged, tranquil or rambunctious—we have the queer experience of falling through the print on the page into something like a dream, an imaginary world so real and convincing that when we happen to be jerked out of it by a call from the kitchen or a knock at the door, we stare for an instant in befuddlement at the familiar room where we sat down, half an hour ago, with our book. To say that we shouldn't react to fictional characters as "real people" is exactly equivalent to saying that we shouldn't be frightened by the things we meet in nightmares.

If it is true that metaphor becomes reality when we read—if it is true, that is, that on encountering the words *whenever it is a damp, drizzly November in my soul, whenever I find myself involuntarily pausing before coffin warehouses, and bringing up the rear of every funeral I meet,* we involuntarily form images of the things represented—then there is nothing inherently wrong with Aristotle's opinion that what chiefly interests us in fiction is characters in action. If it is true that we *do* look at characters in fictions as if they were real, and feel curious about what they will do when their safety is threatened or their wishes are opposed, then the only possible objection to fiction which looks carefully at how things come about—how, given the drives and obsessions of Oedipus, situation *a* in his life leads with murderous inevitability to situation *b*—must be that such study is frivolous. (I would not say, myself, that frivolity is ever an argument against anything; but our object here is to discover whether, on any grounds, causality should be considered an undignified concern.)

What we learn when we look closely at the successive drafts by a writer like Tolstoy—and what one learns if one is oneself a writer who has tested each of his fictional scenes against his experience of how things seem to happen in the world—is that scrutiny of how people act and speak, why people feel precisely the things they do, how weather affects us at particular times, how we respond to some people in ways we would never respond to others, leads to knowledge, sensitivity, and compassion. In fiction we stand back, weigh things as we do not have time to do in life; and the effect of great fiction is to temper real experience, modify prejudice, humanize. One begins a work of fiction with certain clear opinions—for instance, I myself in a recent novel, *October Light,* began with the opinion that traditional New England values are the values we should live by: good workmanship, independence, unswerving honesty, and so on—and one tests those opinions in lifelike situations, puts them under every kind of pressure one can think of, always being fair to the other side, and what one slowly discovers, resisting all the way, is that one's original opinion was oversimple. This is not to say that no opinion stands up, only to say that a simulation of real experience is morally educational.

In this process I describe, the reader is at a disadvantage in that what he has before him is not all the possibilities entertained by the writer and recognized as wrong but only the story the writer eventually came to see as inevitable and right. But the good writer provides his reader, consciously and to some extent mechanically, with a dramatic equivalent of the intellectual process he himself went through. That equivalent is suspense.

Alas, it is even more embarrassing for a serious writer to speak of suspense, these days, than it is to speak of morality or plot. Thirty years ago, when I was an earnest young writer reading books on how to write, I was outraged, I remember, by talk of keeping the reader in suspense. Suspense, it seemed to me—and so those foolish writers on how to write made it seem—was a carrot held out to an idiot donkey, and I had no intention of treating my reader as anything but an equal. But suspense, rightly understood, is a serious business: one presents the moral problem—the character's admirable or unadmirable intent and the pressures of situation working for and against him (what other characters in the fiction feel and need, what imperatives nature and custom urge)—and rather than moving at once to the effect, one tortures the reader with alternative possibilities, translating to metaphor the alternatives the writer has himself considered. Superficially, the delay makes the decision—the climactic action—more thrilling; but essentially the delay makes the decision philosophically significant. Whether the chracter acts rightly or wrongly, his action reflects not simply his nature but his nature as the embodiment of some particular theory of reality and the rejection, right or wrong, of other theories. When the fiction is "tight," as the New Critics used to say, the alternatives are severally represented by the fiction's minor characters, and no charactrer is without philosophical function. True suspense is identical with the Sartrian anguish of choice.

It goes without saying, though I will say it anyway, that even the most lofty and respectable theories of human motivation—from psychiatrists, biologists, theologians, and philosophers—must always be treated by the serious writer as suspect. The writer's sole authority is his imagination. He works out in his imagination what would happen and why, acting out every part himself, making his characters say what he would say himself if he were a young second-generation Italian, then an old Irish policeman, and so on. When the writer accepts unquestioningly someone else's formulation of how and why people behave, he is not thinking but dramatizing some other man's theory: that of Freud, Adler, Laing, or whomever. Needless to say, one may make some theory of motivation one's premise—an idea to be tested. But the final judgment must come from the writer's imagination. True moral fiction is a laboratory experiment too difficult and dangerous to try in the world but safe and important in the mirror image of reality in the writer's mind. Only a madman would murder a sharp old pawn brokeress to test the theory of the superman; but Dostoevski can without harm send his imaginary Raskolnikov into just that experiment in a thoroughly accurate but imaginary St. Petersburg.

The writing of fiction is a mode of thought because by imitating we come to understand the thing we imitate. Fiction is thus a convincing and honest but unverifiable science (in the old sense, knowledge): unverifiable because it depends on the reader's sensitivity and clear sense of how things are, a sense for which we have no tests. Some people claim our basic human nature is vicious, some claim otherwise. The cynic can be shown, by definition, to be a cynic, but he cannot be proved wrong. (So far, unhappily, it cannot even be proved conclusively that he grows ulcers more quickly than do nice people.) Therefore, the kind of knowledge that comes from imitation depends for its quality on the sanity and stability of the imitator. Clearly no absolute standard for sanity and stability exists, but rough estimates are possible. If a writer regularly treats all life bitterly, scorning love, scorning loyalty, scorning decency (according to some standard)—or, to put it another way, if some writer's every remark strikes most or many readers as unfair, cruel, stupid, self-regarding, ignorant, or mad; if he has no good to say of anything or anyone except the character who seems to represent himself; if he can find no pleasure in what happy human beings have found good for centuries (children and dogs, God, peace, wealth, comfort, love, hope, and faith)—then it is safe to hazard that he has not made a serious effort to sympathize and understand, that he has not tried to guess what special circumstances would make him behave, himself, as his enemies behave. We discern the same in more subtle works of art; for instance, when we sense the writer's refusal to be fair to some one or two minor characters, or to some region he dislikes (usually the American Midwest). Whatever some possible divinity might say of such a writer's fictions, the nonomniscient can say this much: he is not using fiction as a mode of thought but merely as a means of preaching his peculiar doctrine. The more appealing or widely shared the doctrine, the more immoral the book. Probably none but his family and closest friends would deny that Richard Nixon is a chump and a grotesque. Nonetheless, Robert Coover's novelistic attack on him—whatever its linguistic and dramatic value, and whatever its values as a warning to democracy—is an aesthetic mistake, an example of immoral fiction.

For Aristotle, imitation was the primary way in which the writer of a fiction makes discoveries. There are other ways. When the writer asks himself, "Would she really say that?" or, "Would he really throw the shoe?" his imagination is working close to the conscious surface. Given a clearly defined character and circumstances, it takes no genius to determine whether or not she would say that or he would throw the shoe. We all have a sense of the probable. If a fierce, violently angry man whose society and family demands eye-for-eye revenge meets his brother's murderer and is invited to tea, any fool can guess that in all likelihood he will not at once accept the invitation and let bygones be bygones. And the same is true in far more subtle situations. When characters behave out of character, readers notice. They may blink the mistake and accept what the writer claims to have happened, but readers do know. If they read on, they do so for lack of something better to read. A strong imagination makes characters do what they would do in real life. A subtler work of the imagination—a subtler way in which the writing of fiction is a morally serious mode of thought—is symbolic association.

There is a game—in the 1950s it used to be played by members of the Iowa Writers' Workshop—called "Smoke." It works as follows. The player who is "it" chooses some famous person with whom everyone playing is surely acquainted (Harry Truman, Marlon Brando, Chairman Mao, Charles DeGaulle, for instance) and tells the other players, "I am a dead American," "I am a living American," "I am a dead Asian," "I am a dead European"; and then each of the other players in turn asks one question of the person who is "it," such as, "What kind of smoke are you?" (cigarette, pipe, cigar—or, more specifically, L&M, Dunhill, White Owl) or "What kind of weather are you?" "What kind of insect are you?" or "What kind of transportation?" The person who is "it" answers not in terms of what kind of smoke his character would *like,* if any, but what kind of smoke he would *be* if, instead of being human, he were a smoke, or what kind of weather, insect, transportation, and so forth, he would be if reincarnated as one of those. Thus, for example, Kate Smith if an insect would be a turquoise beetle; Marlon Brando, if weather, would be sultry and uncertain, with storm warnings out; and as a vehicle of transportation Harry Truman would be (whatever he may in fact have driven) a Model T Ford. What invariably happens when this game is played by fairly sensitive people is that the whole crowd of questioners builds a stronger and stronger feeling of the character, by unconscious association, until finally someone says the right name—"Kate Smith!" or "Chairman Mao!"—and everyone in the room feels instantly that that's right. There is obviously no way to play this game with the reasoning faculty, since it depends on unconscious as-

sociations or intuition; and what the game proves conclusively for everyone playing is that our associations
are remarkably similar. When one of the players falls
into some mistake, for instance, saying that Mr. Brezh-
nev of the U.S.S.R. is a beaver instead of, more properly, a crafty old woodchuck, all the players at the end
of the game are sure to protest, "You misled us when
you said 'beaver.'" The game proves more dramatically than any argument can suggest the mysterious
rightness of a good metaphor—the one requisite for the
poet, Aristotle says, that cannot be taught.

The mainly unconscious or intuitive associations
which show up in the game "Smoke" hint at one of the
ways in which the writing of fiction is a mode of
thought. No one can achieve profound characterization
of a person (or place) without appealing to semi-uncon-
scious associations. To sharpen or intensify a characterization, a writer makes use of metaphor and reinforcing
background—weather, physical objects, animals—
details which either mirror character or give character something to react to. To understand that Marlon
Brando *is* a certain kind of weather is to discover something (though something neither useful nor demonstrable) and in the same instant to communicate something. Thus one of the ways in which fiction thinks is
by discovering deep metaphoric identities. Any given
character may happen to be found, of course, in any setting; but a good writer chooses the setting which makes
character and situation clear. (I do not mean that a character ought to be discovered in the setting that best
reveals him. A man of the mountains may be found in
an automat; but if the man's nature is to be clear to the
reader, the mountains must somehow be implied.)
When fiction is truly a mode of understanding, Raskolnikov can only be a creature of Russia and St. Petersburg; he would not be the same young man at all if

raised in Copenhagen. Given a character who's shy and silent, interested in chemistry, socially retiring but happy with his family, it makes all the difference in the world whether he wears brown or gray. When a writer meets a stranger, the writer should be able to tell quite soon—within reasonable limits—how the stranger's living room is furnished.

What possible moral value can there be, it may be asked, in knowing how a stranger's living room is furnished? The answer is, of course, that it depends on how the knowledge is put to use. We study people carefully for two main reasons: in order to understand them and fully experience our exchange with them, or in order to feel ourselves superior. The first purpose can contribute to art and is natural to art, since the soul of art is celebration and discovery through imitation. The second, perhaps more common purpose, is a mark of petty-mindedness, insecurity, or vice and is the foundation of art that has no value. Both artistic acts, the real and the fraudulent, are obviously egoistic: the true artist is after "glory," as Faulkner said—that is, the pleasure of noble achievement and good people's praise. The false artist is after power and the yawping flattery of his carnivore pack.

The understanding that comes through the discovery of right metaphors can lead the writer to much deeper discoveries, discoveries of the kind made by interpreters of dreams—discoveries, that is, of how one dark metaphor relates to another, giving clues to the landscape of the writer's unconscious and, through these clues, hypotheses on the structure of reality. Pursuit of these clues and hypotheses is the third element—and perhaps the most eerie—in the total creative process which makes fiction a mode of thought.

This is how it works. The writer, let us say, plans his story (some writers do, other writers don't, preferring to make up the story as they go), then writes it in rough draft, employing all his powers of imagination to give clarity and richness, or, to put it another way, make the characters, settings, and events seem real. He knows, for instance, that it is not enough to say *Her father was a drunkard,* since the mere abstract statement does not conjure the image of a drunkard in the reader's mind; instead, the writer must add some concrete image, perhaps some metaphoric expression as well—*She remembered him sitting at the kitchen table, gray as a stone, with his hat on.* Or, again, the writer knows it is not enough to say that some character smoked a pipe; he must, for instance, show the pipe smoke clouding around the face. So the writer continues, character by character, scene by scene, event by event, constantly insisting on concrete images, perhaps backing them with poetic suggestions, until the draft is complete. Many writers—perhaps including some great ones—stop here, but it's a mistake. If the writer looks over his story carefully, again and again, reading aloud, his whole soul as tense as any stalking beast, he will begin, inevitably, to discover odd connections, strange and seemingly inexplicable repetitions. On page 4 he finds the drunkard, gray as a stone, with his hat on; and on page 19 he finds, say, an image of a hushed gray mountain with a hat of low clouds.

In art repetition is always a signal, intentional or not, and when the moral artist finds in his work some such accident of language as the one I've just fabricated, he refuses to rest until he has somehow understood—or can emotionally confirm—the accident. He asks himself consciously—perhaps writes it down on a slip of yellow paper—"Why is this particular drunken father like this particular mountain?" Occasionally the question remains stubbornly unanswerable, and the writer, convinced by the prickling of his scalp that the mysterious equation is significant, God knows how, will simply let it stand, or will perhaps reinforce it with some further related image which feels equally right, God knows why. There's nothing essentially wrong in this. At a certain point in human thought, rationality breaks down and can speak to us only of the mundane. But whether or not the writer can finally answer the questions his writing fishes up from the bog of the unconscious, he asks them carefully, again and again. He reevaluates, in the light of the messages he's received from the swamp, all that his fiction has labored to maintain. If he has claimed, for instance, that a particular character is sterile and empty, yet accidents of language or of image-echo have secretly identified that character with forces of fecundity and fullness, the writer tries the hypothesis that his first opinion was wrong. He plays part against part, hunting out each part's secrets, until something clicks.

In short, the discoveries of "epiphanies" in great fiction are not fully planned in advance: they evolve. So Anna, to Tolstoy's surprise, commits suicide, though he'd been brooding on that mangled young body on the tracks for years. So Mrs. Eustace, to Trollope's astonishment, steals her own diamonds.

This is not, for the moral writer, a mere device, a way of coming up with interesting surprises for the audience. It reflects a fundamental conviction of the artist that the mind does not impose structures on reality (as existentialists claim)—arbitrarily maintaining now this, now that—but rather, as an element of total reality—a capsulated universe—discovers, in discovering itself, the world. The artist's theory, as revealed by his method (however artists may deny it), is that the things he thinks when he thinks most dispassionately—not "objectively," quite, but with passionate commitment to discovering whatever may happen to be true (not merely proving that some particular thing is true)—that the ideas the artist gets, to put it another way, when he thinks with the help of the full artistic method, are absolutely valid, true not only for himself but for everyone, or at least for all human beings. And some artists would go further. Tolstoy never doubted his understanding of dogs and horses; Hemingway believed he could communicate with bears; Henry James knew the minds of ghosts.

To someone who has never written real poetry or fiction, all of this may seem doubtful; but it is a method that can be studied wherever great writers have left sketches and consecutive drafts. That the method is still common is easily verified: simply ask writers how they work, if you can get them to tell the truth. The method is not always as conscious as I've made it seem, of course. Some writers may insist, as Bernard Malamud does, that they simply keep tinkering until everything seems right. But however the given writer expresses it, this feeling out of the fiction's implications, this refusal to let the fiction go until it has proved itself a closed and self-sustaining system, an alternative reality, an organism, this is the true writer's check on himself and his road to understanding. It is here that fake art hopelessly breaks down. One does not achieve the dense symbolic structure of *Death in Venice* or *The Sound and the Fury* by planning it all out on butcher paper, though one does make careful plans. True writing, as William Gaddis says in *JR*, is

like living with a God damned invalid . . . eyes follow you around the room wave his God damned stick figure out what the hell he wants, plump the God damned pillow change bandage read aloud move a clause around wipe his chin new paragraph. . . .

I will mention one last check on fiction's honesty: tradition. No writer imagines he exists in a literary void. Though writers rarely read as widely as do critics—partly because writers can afford to be critical, throwing out books because of annoying little flaws of conception or execution—it is nevertheless true that writers would not be what they are if they didn't have a liking for books. A particular writer may read no one but George Gissing or, perhaps, Aristophanes; but he knows full well that one of the things he's doing when he writes is laboring to achieve an effect at least somewhat similar to effects he has gotten out of other people's books. When a writer begins a story *It was winter of the year 1833. A large man stepped out of a doorway,* that writer has a literary tradition in mind, and part of his purpose is to be—besides interesting and original—true to the tradition (or anyway steadily aware of it). When he begins a story *She was no longer afraid of the long drive home,* he has another distinct tradition in mind, and still another when he begins *"Henry, come clean off them boots," Mrs. Cobb called out the woodshed door.* The medium of literary art is not language but language plus the writer's experience and imagination and, above all, the whole of the literary tradition he knows. Just as the writer comes to discoveries by studying the accidental implications of what he's said, he comes to discoveries by trying to say what he wants to say without violating the form or combination of forms to which he's committed. It isn't true that, as New Critics used to say with great confidence, "Form is content." The relationship between the two is complex almost beyond description. It *is* true, as Wallace Stevens said, that " a change of style is a change of subject."

The process of discovery through a struggle with tradition is most obvious in the retelling of some traditional myth. In my own retelling of the story of *Jason and Medea,* I shackled myself with one basic rule: I would treat the same events treated in the past (by Apollonius and Euripides), making sure that the characters said approximately the same things, performed the same actions, and made the same friends and enemies among men and gods; but all that happened I would try to understand with a modern sensibility (granting the existence of gods as forces), asking myself how *I*, in these situations, could say and do what these antique figures did. In what sense could I understand the Sirens, or Circe, or the Golden Fleece? What would make me, as a modern woman (as a writer, one claims androgyny), kill my children? The result of this process is that one gets the impression, rightly or wrongly, that one has to some extent penetrated what is common in human experience throughout time; and since again and again the ancient poets seem right, and "modern sensibility" seems a fool's illusion, one gets the impression that one has come to grasp, more firmly than before, fragments of the ancient poets' wisdom.

The same process is at work, less obviously, when one decides to write a "gothic," a murder mystery, a family saga, or a country yarn, and at work much more subtly when one commits oneself to a conventional realistic novel—or, for that matter, to a serious poem in tetrameter quatrains without rhyme. What has gone before exerts its light pressure, teasing the mind just as tarot cards do toward queer new visions of the familiar.

Such are my arguments for what I have described as "the best kind of fiction." I am convinced that all the arts work in a somewhat similar fashion, though I am not qualified to make the case. Needless to say, I don't mean in all this to be unduly sober-minded. I have nothing against limericks, tales of boys and dogs, or the earlier installments of *Star Trek*, nothing against canvas stretched between two mountains to make us more aware of the beauty of the valley now blocked off, nothing much even against the junky electronic music on "All Things Considered." I do object strongly to the cult of sex and violence, and more strongly yet to the cult of cynicism and despair, not that I recommend censorship. I am convinced that, once the alarm has been sounded, good art easily beats out bad, and that the present scarcity of first-rate art does not follow from a sickness of society but the other way around—unless, possibly, the two chase each other's tails. In the past few decades we have shaken off, here in America, the childish naivete and prudishness we see in, for instance, movies of the thirties and forties, in which the killers say "Jeez" and the reporters say "Gosh," but in our pursuit of greater truth we have fallen to the persuasion that the cruellest, ugliest thing we can say is likely to be the truest. Real art has never been fooled by such nonsense: real art has internal checks against it.

Real art creates myths a society can live instead of die by, and clearly our society is in need of such myths. What I claim is that such myths are not mere hopeful fairy tales but the products of careful and disciplined thought; that a properly built myth is worthy of belief, at least tentatively; that working at art is a moral act; that a work of art is a moral example; and that false art can be known for what it is if one remembers the rules. The black abyss stirs a certain fascination, admittedly, or we would not pay so many artists so much money to keep staring at it. But the black abyss is merely life as it is or as it soon may become, and staring at it does nothing, merely confirms that it is there. It seems to me time that artists start taking that fact as pretty thoroughly established.

2

Moral Criticism

I‍T'S a little absurd, as the cartoonist David Levine has sometimes mentioned, that criticism should be the business of specialists. It ought not to require years of education for a man to pronounce judgment on a blank canvas presented as a finished work of art, or knowledge of all music from Bach to Robert Helps for a man to assess the aesthetic significance of blowing up a grand piano. There are advantages, admittedly, to allowing among the walks of life the specialization "criticism," since most of us—artists and other honest laborers—have no time to check out every new movement, desperately hunting for just one somewhere that isn't foolishness. Critics would be useful people to have around if they would simply do their work, carefully and thoughtfully assessing works of art, calling our attention to those worth noticing, and explaining clearly, sensibly, and justly why others need not take up our time. It is of course true that a man who has nothing to do all day long but look at new paintings, listen to new music, or read new books, has an advantage over the rest of us. He can, theoretically, tune his perceptions to a very fine pitch, and he has a better chance than we do of knowing, for what it's worth, which work is truly original and which mere imitation, which work is technically accomplished and which mere yawp, which work is relevant and morally beneficial in terms of the deep-seated diseases of the age and which mere shoddy propaganda, fashionable pseudodoxy, ill-considered rant, or indecent exposure.

This is not, for the most part, what critics do. Critics in recent decades have managed greatly to simplify their work—the accurate assessment of aesthetic objects—by elaborating theories on why they would be wrong to do it. Most critics would probably agree, at least privately, that an important work of art is at least some of the following: 1) aesthetically interesting, 2) technically accomplished, and 3) intellectually massive. A few might even be persuaded that a work cannot be intellectually massive and yet patently wrong, asserting what is false or celebrating what the best and most humane would despise. The trouble is, judging these matters is rather difficult. What, aside from whim, makes aesthetic interest? (Is Genet's theater of assault aesthetically interesting? Is John Cage's *Silence?* Is a painting by Reubens? What have the three in common?) Again, what do we mean, exactly, by "technically accomplished?" Does technique include mental agility or cleverness, as in the thinking up of a conceptual—and physically nonexistent—work of art? If Robert Rauschenberg erases parts of another artist's work, is his erasing "better" than someone else's? As for intellectual massiveness, isn't it presumptuous of the critic to pretend to judge? And anyway, are the paintings of Miro "intellectually massive"? Are they "true" or "life-giving," therefore moral?

At the thought of asking these questions all over

again every time one looks at a new work of art—or at the thought, worse yet, of looking at each new work with completely innocent eyes, trying to understand and appreciate it in its own terms—the usual, bad critic's mind boggles. What the bad critic needs is some handy formula; and for most of this century the central question for both popular and scholarly critics has therefore been: What is the simplest formula I can hope to get away with?

The first great evasion—though it was not originally intended as an evasion—was the New Criticism, which studied works of art as if they existed independent of the universe, outside time and culture, as self-sufficient organisms. That school of course served as an invaluable corrective to the almost universal nineteenth-century evasion, which avoided talking about the work by talking, instead, about the man who created it; and thanks to what was healthy in the New Critical approach—thanks, also, to its seeming verifiability—New Criticism threatened for a time to consume the world. A number of equally ingenious evasions rose in furious reaction—Marxist criticism, generic criticism, various forms of historical criticism, the present fad of structuralist criticism, destructionist criticism, and the safest, easiest approach of all, "hermaneutics," or opinion, bastard grandson of the eighteenth century's rule of taste.

None of these schools really qualifies as criticism—though some, ingeniously applied, give a valuable start—first, because they're all too neat, too theoretical, too "scientific" to deal with so lively and unpredictable a creature as art, and second, because they ignore the very essence of art, which is emotional affirmation. Take the matter of neatness first.

What criticism ought to be is the business of asking, as I. A. Richards phrased the questions fifty years ago,

"What gives the experience of reading a certain poem its value? How is this experience better than another? Why prefer this picture to that? In which ways should we listen to music so as to receive the most valuable moments? Why is one opinion about works of art not as good as another? . . . What *is* a picture, a poem, a piece of music? How can experiences be compared? What is value?" [13] A moment's thought shows that the usefulness of these questions is precisely that the critic, thinking about different works of art, can never answer them in the same way twice. Art does the same things, age after age, but because art deals with impressions, feelings, and because it will not submit to the petty demands of intellect, it is forever shifting ground, changing its means, sneaking up from behind. James Joyce, working in what may fairly be described as an innocent age, makes heavy use of symbolism, knowing the reader will catch it only subliminally, so that it will deepen rather than intellectualize his fiction. Today when we read *Dubliners* (though it's less tue, I think, of the later books), the symbols stand out like wounds; that is, what was subtle and innovative in *Dubliners* is now obvious. So today the serious writer must subvert his reader's intelligence, getting to what matters some other way. It's of course true that we do find symbols in the work of John Hawkes, John Barth, Thomas Pynchon, William Gass, or Douglas Woolf; but Hawkes' symbols slip and slide, transmogrify, turn inside out; Barth's symbols are as open as jokes; Pynchon's symbols are Platonic inexpressibles (for instance, the *SS* of *Gravity's Rainbow*), mythic and mystical summaries of everything, not pegs on which to hang argument but, instead, the innumerable disguises which mask what can only be described as the central mystery. Gass uses symbols in a variety of ways, so their meaning is seldom obvious at a glance; in Woolf, symbols become comic characters in a tragic farce.

Because change is a necessity of art's existence, every form of criticism which studies works of art "objectively," by some single standard involving means, not ends, is wrong from the beginning. It was in acknowledgment of this fact that Northrop Frye wrote, some years ago, that "we do not have to confine our contact with literature to purely disinterested and esthetic responses. We should mutilate our literary experience if we did, and mutilations of experience designed merely to keep a theory consistent indicate something wrong with the theory." [14] But this did not prevent Frye from saying:

The fundamental act of criticism is a disinterested response to a work of literature in which all one's beliefs, engagements, commitments, prejudices, stampedings of pity and terror, are ordered to be quiet. We are now dealing with the imaginative, not the existential, with "let this be," not with "this is," and no work of literature is better by virtue of what it says than any other work. Such a disinterested response takes rigorous discipline to attain, and many, even among skilled critics, never consistently attain it. But the fact that it is there to be attained can hardly be disputed. [15]

Frye is claiming, as the New Criticism regularly claimed, that what counts in literature is not what it says, what it affirms and promulgates, but only how well it works as a self-contained, organic whole busy doing whatever it does. There's some truth in that, of course, but the position leaves out art's primary business: direct or indirect (ironic) affirmation. Frye's position—all but universal in the past few decades—refuses to investigate why *The Iliad* is the greatest single poem in our tradition, or why Shakespeare at his worst is better than de Sade at his best. It shrugs off such questions because it thinks it knows the answer: beauty is truth and truth is relative. As Frye has it, "To go beyond this point would take us into a world of higher belief, a view of the human situation so broad that the whole of literature would illustrate it. . . . Beauty and truth may be attributes of good writing, but if the writer deliberately aims at truth, he is likely to find that what he has hit is the didactic; if he deliberately aims at beauty, he is likely to find that what he has hit is the insipid."[16]

Judging technique, analyzing the artist's manipulation of such categories as unity, consistency, and appropriateness or decorum, is a good deal easier than judging art, but the technical judgment is sometimes relevant, sometimes not. This is not to say that artists should be followed blindly or that all we have learned about technique should be scrapped. Insofar as technique is relevant to the purpose of the artist at a given time, insofar as asking about technical perfection is not out-and-out frigidity (as it often is in the case of *Moby Dick* or Malory's *Morte D'Arthur*), our understanding of technique and our ability to evaluate it enhance our appreciation of what the artist has done. But even in conspicuously technical art, no serious viewer, listener, or reader—certainly no artist—is indifferent to whether the work in front of him is not just well-made but in some sense noble, fit to last. It is true that we can leave questions of evaluation for later, can cross our fingers as reviewers are forever doing and hopefully call new writers "gifted," comforting ourselves with the opinion that nobody can really tell. But it is self-delusion. A good book is one that, for its time, is wise, sane, and magical, one that clarifies life and tends to improve it. The qualification *for its time* is important: at certain historical moments, wisdom is rage and sanity is madness. At times when reasonableness and goodness are live options, an artist ought to be reasonable and good, speaking calmly, as if from the mountaintop; at other times, as in Jacobean England and some parts of the world at the present time, it may be that one cannot support those same lofty ideals except with dynamite. Either way, true art treats ideals, affirming and clarifying the Good, the True, and the Beautiful. Ideals are art's *ends;* the rest is methodology. True criticism, what I am calling "moral criticism," may speak of technique and sometimes ought to, but its ultimate concern is with ends. For the real importance of literary technique—as I've explained in my remarks on the process by which one achieves moral fiction—is that it helps the writer check himself and zero in on truth.

There seems to be some question, these days, as to whether those old words the Good, the True, and the Beautiful have any meaning. If not, the kind of criticism I advocate is nonsense. Let me say a few words, then—borrowing from the argument of Aquinas and Ockham—in defense of those old ideas.

The Good, the True, and the Beautiful are not, as everyone knows, things that exist in the way llamas do, but values which exist when embodied and, furthermore, recognized as embodied (by someone who speaks English; otherwise they would be called by other names). They are values by definition, and by inspection not relative values but relative absolute values, like health. The term *relative absolute* is not, as it may seem, double-talk. We can legitimately distinguish between "relatively good health" (an eighty-year-old man with a case of pneumonia but doing very well) and "perfect health," an ideal condition—a conceptual abstraction—approached by an eighty-year-old man without physical complaints. By the relative absolute "perfect health" we mean not perfect health for a particular man and not the indestructibility of some posited god but the abstract idea of physical and mental soundness represented by all healthy people, animals, and plants. We can speak in the same fashion of physiological and social well-being. As long as evolution meets no dead end, there is always the possibility that today's relative absolute of health may not be tomorrow's. For example, if man develops through mutation a heightened sensitivity to psychic phenomena, the standard of "perfect" mental health for the human species will, I suppose, change. Thus the ideal state of well-being for the human body and spirit is approximately absolute at any given point in time but relative with respect to the total history of mankind. Needless to say, perfect mental health in human beings as they are now constructed is not a fixed, ideal state but an almost totally satisfactory adjustment; but this does not mean that any man who can muddle through, however monstrous his environment, is healthy. Conceived abstractly, the relative absolute "perfect mental health" is the highest level of understanding possible in man, a level unattainable in adverse environments like Amin's Uganda or Hitler's Germany because they severely limit free choice and available options. True health of this kind is therefore partly a product of lucky circumstances, which means, normally—as R. G. Collingwood showed in *The New Leviathan*—a product of civilization. The Good for man, which rightly understood cannot be divorced from what is good for his society and environment, is by another formulation (whenever action is called for) the *moral*. Morality is the body, or engine, of the Good. The Good is form: morality is function; and form *is* function, or at any rate form can no more exist independent of function than time can exist without a natural or man-made clock.

Morality, then, describes actions or preparations for action (psychological actions); and since the possible number of actions in the universe is unlimited—as is the number of possible situations from which actions may proceed and take their tone—morality is infinitely complex, too complex to be *knowable* and far too complex to be reduced to any code, which is why it is suitable matter for fiction, which deals in understanding, not knowledge. This does not mean that morality is out of our reach but only that it is beyond the strictly analytical process which leads to knowing. We should also observe here that absolute morality is not practical, like the multiplication tables, even though it is valuable and within the grasp of human understanding. We can argue about knowledge (e.g., $7 \times 4 = 28$) by challenging the analysis out of which it comes; but to dispute understanding is largely futile. One man's understanding is as good as another's not because each is equally valid but because right understanding does not submit to any proof. If Mr. Smith empathizes well with strangers and Mr. Perkins is convinced that everyone is out to steal his shoes, Mr. Smith's understanding is more correct than Mr. Perkins', but it gives Mr. Perkins no good reason to stop glancing at his feet. Thus healthy society is pluralistic, allowing every man his opinion as long as the opinion does not infringe on the rights of others. This compromise morality is sometimes—as in the writings of Kierkegaard—called ethics and distinguished from true morality or, as we misleadingly call it, private morality. The trouble with pluralism, not that anyone in his right mind wants to get rid of it, is that it tends to undermine man's ability to believe in true morality, to go out in defiance of mere positive law, like Antigone, and do what the gods require. I need not take space here for a full defense of the idea of the moral; a shortcut will be sufficient.[17]

If the Good seems relative in our dealings with adults, it seems less so in our dealings with children. No one who has worked with children, who has watched healthy and unhealthy families in action, or clearly remembers his own childhood, will be tempted to deny that wanton cruelty, consistent indifference, betrayal, habitual insincerity, and the like do noticeable psychological harm. Under right treatment, the child thrives: when his talents are recognized and encouraged, when his love gets a fair return, when his antisocial inclinations are discouraged without meanness, preserving him from later, necessarily fiercer discouragement, the child learns security, feels a minimum of self-hatred, and, in a word, matures. Under wrong treatment, the child becomes a psychological cripple. To say that no one can spell out in detail the exact rules of ideal child-rearing is not to say that the ideal does not exist for our intuition or that it is not sometimes approached by good parents.

Just as there are ideal patterns of behavior between adults and children, there are ideal patterns between adults and adults, though the latter are even more difficult than the former to achieve in practice. To adopt an ancient formulation, healthy relationships between adults are characterized by sympathy and trust and are supported on both sides by maturity; which is to say, by freedom from those selfish passions which (as Spinoza pointed out) inhibit understanding. Perhaps such relationships are rare—I am personally not too sure of that—but at all events, the ideal is possible to approach.

Understood in this way, the Good (the goal of the moral) does not, in Frye's words, "take us into a world of higher belief, a view of the human condition so broad that the whole of literature would illustrate it." On the contrary, it presents a goal for the human condition here in this world, a conceptual abstraction of our actual experience of moments of good in human life; it is the essential subject of all literature, even of a strict imagist poem which asserts nothing but the value of seeing, but not all literature illustrates it: badly thought out literature obscures it, and nihilistic literature perniciously denies it. As for Frye's assertion that the writer who deliberately aims at "truth" (he means moral principle) "is likely to find that what he has hit is the didactic," we are required to answer that the particular writer's incompetence is no reason for ruling out the Good as a value in literature. Didacticism inevitably simplifies morality and thus misses it. One of the inconveniences of the writer's business is that it is his job to hit or at least come close to what he aims at. The view of the Good which I have presented denies (or at any rate avoids) the metaphysical assumption, seen in Hegel, for instance, that there are properties, subsistent entities, which attach to existent particulars (boy scouts, say, or missionaries) but might without absurdity be supposed to attach to nothing. The idea of an imperishable form for the Good has always been appealing, since it keeps the Good from changing with governments and hair styles; but actually we need not invent ghosts to keep things relatively stable. To say that by the Good a human being can mean only the human good—the only good he has any hope of understanding, that is, any hope of intuitively grasping—is not to say that the Good is a matter of opinion. To deduce from personal and cultural experience that the idea is there to be discovered, whether or not any man will ever have the wit to discover it, is to claim for the idea of the Good the same verifiable efficacy, and in that sense "reality," that we claim for the structure of a properly functioning molecule. The Good is existential in the sense that its existence depends upon man's, not in the sense that it can be defined adequately by a clod's personal assertion.

But does art really have anything to do with the Good? Most of modern criticism has followed the lead of I. A. Richards in his *Principles of Literary Criticism*—though Richards himself later abandoned his early position and became, in fact, something of a mystic. Working out of deterministic psychological theory, Richards in *Principles* identifies our sense of the Good in art with our discovery, as we watch a play, of a momentarily adequate psychological stance or "attitude," not really a matter of belief or moral affirmation but rather one of satisfied expectation, tension release—in short, aesthetic pleasure. Our relief at having overcome some obstacle to personality balance, he says, gives us

the peculiar sense of ease, of restfulness, of free unimpeded activity, and the feeling of acceptance, of something more positive than acquiescence. This feeling is the reason why such states may be called beliefs. They share this feeling with, for example, the state which follows the conclusive answering of a question. Most attitude-adjustments which are successful possess it in some degree, but those which are very regular and familiar, such as sitting down to meat or stretching out in bed, naturally tend to lose it. But when the required attitude has been long needed, where its coming is unforeseen and the manner in which it is brought about complicated and inexplicable, where we know no more than that formerly we were unready and that now we are ready for life in some particular phase, the feeling which results may be intense.[18]

The psychological mechanics here are interesting and no doubt have, metaphorically at least, some validity; but Richards' denial that the Good exists as a physiological effect is unconvincing. The concept of the Good—our *belief* in the Good—comes from outside us as well as from within. When the brain is at its most creative, when the so-called theta waves are efficiently "scanning," as neurologists say, they are scanning in order to find *something*. The weakness in Richards' account in *Principles* is his failure to distinguish clearly between knowledge and understanding as alternative approaches to—or ways of scanning for—outside reality. It is true that it is always difficult to say exactly what real art "means"—exactly what our "attitude adjustment" adds up to—but not because the process which leads to affirmation is less precise than that which leads to "the conclusive answering of a question." It is a different process. Though the distinction between knowledge and understanding may seem abstruse, it is one we recognize in everday speech: I can I "understand" you, having *felt* the coherence of your speech, gestures, and behavior, but we all agree that no human being can really "know" another one. If I say I "know" you, I mean I know some of the classifications which help to identify you: your name, features, occupation, age, religious persuasion, and so on.

Knowledge may or may not lead to belief; understanding always does, since to believe one understands a complex situation is to form at least a tentative theory of how one ought to behave in it. If fiction contains lifelike characters, then, and if in the process of reading we come to understand them and worry about them, feeling suspense because their ways of behaving, right or wrong, may get them into trouble, and if in reading a work of fiction we anticipate events and hope that characters will act in one way and not another, bringing about happiness and moral satisfaction, not misery and shame, then fiction is concerned with the Good.

The conclusive answering of a question has to do not with the Good but with the True. Whereas we intuit the Good, we approach the unattainable and thus relative absolute "Truth" through reason. At the end of each process we have of course learned something, which means we have gotten control over something and are stronger, less vulnerable than we were before. It is this similarity that leads to confusion of the two. Apprehended strictly as feeling states, the two emotions of release, knowledge and understanding, may indeed be indistinguishable. Richards called attention to one classic situation in which understanding has precisely the emotional effect of knowledge and indeed would be knowledge if only one could prove how one arrived at it—as one never can when imagination is the source. People with exceptional color sense, Richards says, seem to judge most accurately whether two colors are the same, or have or have not some definite harmonic relation to one another, not by attentive optical comparison but by the general emotional or organic reaction which the colors evoke when simply ganced at. Obviously the conviction "this yellow is the same as that one" feels like knowledge, though technically it's belief. By the same sure imaginative faculty some people (especially women, we're often told) are able to grasp "intuitively" the coherent personality of certain people the first time they see them, so that they "know" enough at once to be afraid of them or how to mimic them. It goes without saying that understanding, like knowledge, can grow, rising higher and higher toward the absolute. An obvious example is the growth of understanding between friends with the passing of time.

I said earlier that the Good is a relative absolute that cannot be approached except by the imagination because our understanding of it arises out of our experience of an infinite number of particular situations. Let us now look more closely at Truth and Beauty.

Truth is that which can be known for certain, an object of reason and analysis. Absolute Truth is all that could be known by an omniscient mind, and insofar as the universe contains voluntary agents and a random evolution of everything from brute matter to conscious thought, Truth is relative in the same manner as is Goodness. Truth, in this sense, though by no means unimportant, is normally the lowest concern of fiction. Accurate imitation of the world gives pleasure, and the pleasure can be intense when we encounter accurate imitation by a writer with a gift for noticing in conventional settings precisely those details that most people miss, or a gift for choosing to describe those settings that others would never have though to describe. One thinks, for example, of Ross MacDonald's treatment of shoddy California motels, of Balzac's Paris, Dickens' London, or Zane Grey's West. On the other hand, a writer's indifference to actuality can be highly offensive, as when he ignorantly fakes a battle scene, a New York neighborhood, or the details of his character's vocation. We value truth in fiction as we value it in realistic drawing: an inspired metaphor which shows us exactly how a certain character shakes his head, or a selection of details which vividly calls back New England country life in 1934, can make an ordinary novel extraordinary. No story or novel can dispense entirely with truth; nevertheless truth is not the highest concern of fiction. Though it matters that the descriptions of locale in Mann's *Death in Venice* are accurate and can be verified, so that the fiction's symbolic power has a resonance that is missing from, say, Bunin's "The Gentleman from San Francisco," it does not matter absolutely. The main value of Mann's careful recording of literal detail is that the truth of place, like the "truth" in Mann's analysis of characters (the precision and good judgment), gives increased weight, increased authority, a certain metaphysical conviction to his probing of larger questions, the struggle of order and disorder, of form and substance—the roles, in the life of old Aschenbach, of the Beautiful and the Good. There is no such truth of setting (or very little) in *Beowulf*, and no one cares: the moral causality is inexorable, and that's enough. To put this another way, truth is useful in realistic art but is much less necessary to the fabulous; when it appears it serves chiefly as a means and only trivially as an end. Truth is a requisite of Wordsworth's part of the *Lyrical Ballads*, but where verisimilitude gives way, as in the poetry of Coleridge, to poetic voice and the willing suspension of disbelief for the moment, truth—verifiable fact—plays a smaller part.

It may seem that truth has a larger role in expository verse—for example, in Pope's *Essay on Criticism*, wherein truth, accuracy, seems a central concern—but the subject of Pope's essay is aesthetic judgment and belief, not fact; and in any event, if someone should ask why the *Essay* is not in plain prose, which might perhaps be clearer, more scientific, we would no doubt answer impatiently that in prose it wouldn't be the same at all—it's the verse that provides the delight. It's difficult to describe what emotion it is that we feel as we read Pope's verse essays, but surely it's clear that the puns, the neat paradoxes, the rhythmic jokes, the ingenious rhyming—in a word, the "wit"—all together establish in the reader a certain psychological "set," the feeling that belongs to reading Pope. Another slightly different feeling belongs to reading Butler's *Hudibras*, another to Oliver Wendell Holmes. All of this is to say that when talking about art we use the word *truth* in two ways: to mean that which is factually accurate or logically valid, on the one hand, and, on the other, to mean that which does not feel like lying. What does not feel like lying is that which is true to the essential nobility of the writer's soul, that which expresses what is purest and best in his personality, in which all healthy human beings have a share. Its effect is to conjure by incantation what the art receiver may have lost touch with, his own best nature, his affirmations.

Like the True and the Good, the Beautiful has often been treated as a subsistent entity immanent in particulars but ultimately transcendent. So Hegel treats it. Poe disagreed:

When, indeed, men speak of Beauty, they mean, precisely, not a quality, as is supposed, but an effect—they refer, in short, just to that intense and pure elevation of soul—not of intellect, or of the heart . . .—which is experienced in consequence of contemplating "the beautiful." [19]

Given Poe's idea of art as a conveying of "impressions," it seems that he does not quite mean, here, that "the beautiful" does not exist, or that it exists only in the eye of the beholder; what he more nearly means is that as vibrations are not sound except when they strike an eardrum, so beauty *comes alive* in the mind of the beholder. Beauty, he says, involves neither intellect (which pursues the True) nor moral feeling (which pursues the Good; but the "soul." What *soul* means, here or anywhere else, must be left to intuition. For the moment it is enough to note that Richards' idea of Beauty (in *Principles*) would not meet with Poe's approval. Richards, too, sees Beauty primarily as a quality of mind; he considers it an exalted form of pleasure, the comforting satisfaction of expectation. Richards begins by showing, rightly, that expectation is an act. Given reason to expect a certain thing (having walked into a museum, for example) we flex our muscles, so to speak, to the work of waiting. Given satisfaction, we feel a relaxation, a new comfort, and this we give the name of Beauty.

But Poe is more convincing. The pleasure is of a special kind: the pleasure we get—at least where art is concerned—from seeing a difficult task accomplished 1) elegantly and 2) without shortcuts or falsification. When the writer goes wrong, fooling himself, cheapening the experience, we wince; when he slips skillfully through every difficulty—as Italo Calvino almost always does, or John Fowles, or, on his smaller canvas Guy Davenport—never sinking to the tawdry or false, never presenting us with anything to which our infinitely complex chemistry must say, *No! You lie!* (exactly as, in another situation, our chemistry says at the merest glance, "No, that's a different shade of blue"), our arrival at understanding is accompanied by that particular feeling of release, of "freedom from the limits of Time and Space," as Pound said, which we call the sense of the beautiful.

Beauty, then, is the truth of feeling (cf. Poe's word, *soul*). The artist, like other people, senses this coherent truth of feeling at certain moments of his life; unlike other people, he works his way back to those moments by formal means, recreating them in his painting, symphonic suite, or novel, embodying truth of feeling both in the overall form of his work (an emotionally felt-out right arrangement of an assembly of feelings) and line by line, emotion by emotion. Beauty has, in itself, nothing to do with either the True or the Good. The salience on a Gothic capital is not too long or too short, too fat or too thin, in any moral sense but only in the sense that it feels wrong and must have felt wrong to the artist as well. If it did not feel wrong to the artist, then he had a bad system of emotions. Similarly, the tirades against rote-religion and the like in Tolstoy's late *Resurrection* are ugly not because of their implicit fascism but because they show warped emotion. The immorality is incidental. Frost was right in claiming that the choice of each image in a poem is a moral choice, but only because it is the poet's obligation to make no bad choice if he can help it. The immorality of an inept poet is like that of a sleeping guard or a drunken bus driver.

Truth, Goodness, and Beauty are thus, in varying degrees, the fundamental concerns of art and therefore ought to be the fundamental concerns of criticism. Otherwise criticism must be irrelevant. Where Truth is a major concern of the artist (as in Hellenic sculpture or the historical, psychological, or sociological novel), the critic's first concern should be the question, Is the artist correct? Wherever Goodness is a relevant criterion (as in all novels), it is one which ought to be applied. As for Beauty, it should not be conceived only as a matter of technique (the harmonious balance of unity and multeity, for instance) but as the effect of emotional honesty as well, balance as an expression of the artist's personality maturely realized, for the moment, in the work of art. This does not rule out honesty achieved by tortuous indirection. Critical standards built on the premise that art is primarily technique rather than correctness of vision—built on the premise that every artist has his own private notion of reality and all notions are equal—cannot deal with important but clumsy artists (Dostoevski, Poe, Lawrence, Dreiser, Faulkner) except by emphasizing what is minor in their work; and they cannot deal with limited men who are masters of technique (Pound, Roethke) except by bloating their reputations and hurrying them down the road to eventual oblivion. A beautiful work of art—Proust's *Remembrance of Things Past*, for example—is better than its creator but also *is* its creator, Marcel Proust transmuted from neurotic and spiteful invalid to heroic man. The beauty of the book in turn infects the reader, whose increased value glorifies the book. Wallace Stevens was right; it's in our lives—or nowhere—that beauty is immortal.

True criticism is, at least some of the time, morally judgmental. I do not mean that to be a proper critic one must bray like an ass or apply the same standards to *The Odyssey* and Stephen Becker's *The Chinese Bandit.* I mean only that when a novel or poem, a film or play, achieves some noble end, the critic should not hesitate to mention the fact and comment, insofar as possible, on how the effect is achieved; and when, as much more commonly happens, a literary work cheats or lies or achieves its right or wrong ends unfairly, or celebrates what ought to be scorned, or mocks what should be praised, the critic should say what has gone wrong and should point out why.

The trouble with the kind of criticism I recommend is that it's difficult. Anyone can talk about tensions, paradoxes, or unique vision. Anyone can impose magic words like "unmediated vision" (Geoffrey Hartman) or "interpretive choice" (Stanley Fish) and rewrite the poems to fit the magic. Not everyone is capable of judging the moral maturity or emotional honesty of Gunther Grass or Robert Creeley. Nevertheless, to avoid such judgments is to treat art as a plaything. It is not. It may not really legislate for humanity—an idea still worth trying—but whether it is heard or not, it is civilization's single most significant device for learning what must be affirmed and what must be denied. A writer writes a novel, a poet writes a poem, to find out what he can honestly maintain, not just with his head but with all his nature. He gives it to readers not only to delight them and instruct them but also to support them if they are the right kind of people already and stir doubts if they're not. We live, necessarily, in a jungle of half-truths and outright lies: if we didn't we'd be forever at one another's throats. Some lies we tell out of politeness, some because we feel foolish contradicting opinions widely accepted in our time. But telling familiar lies does not make them true. Art is our way of keeping track of what we know and have known, secretly, from the beginning.

It is precisely because art affirms values that it is important. The trouble with our present criticism is that criticism is, for the most part, not important. It treats the only true magic in the world as though it were done with wires.

3

The Artist As Critic

THOUGH art is one of civilization's chief defenses, the hammer that tries to keep the trolls in their place, and though artists are by nature makers, not destroyers, the artist ought not to be too civilized—that is to say, too meekly tolerant—especially toward other artists, who may be trolls in disguise. The artist's trade is essentially an unreasonable one, though he may reason about it. However reasonably he may talk, if the artist believes in what he's doing he cannot help but feel strongly, at least some of the time, about what he believes to be fraudulent art. If he can stand to do so, he should speak out, especially now, when so much art is fake. He should defend—with dignity but as belligerently as necessary—the artists whose work he values and attack with equal belligerence all that he hates. No one can do it for him, because the artist's character—the whole complex of his ideas and emotions—is his final authority on what is, and what is not, art. Except insofar as they are really artists, critics have, finally, no authority at all. Professional critics know about art pre-

147

cisely because they stand back from it as the artist cannot do. As a result they're judges of technique, apologists for some artist's vision, or abstract moral philosophers.

The music critic Barry Farrell once summed up the problem every decent critic faces when art makes one of its sudden, seemingly idiotic leaps, changing all the rules. He tells of his painful experience at a concert of "new works" by composers who refuse to compose, and he remarks, "Then, in the din, an unwelcome thought crossed my mind: *none of these people was hearing what I heard.* Here I was, with pad and earnest pencil, straining my ear to judge the talents of a musician who only rubbed balloons together. Did he rub badly? Well? Was it pretty? What did it mean?"

Only the true artist can know for sure, by the test of his emotions, whether some new, surprising venture that declares itself art is in fact art. That is what makes art such a nuisance, and why the role of the artist is so easy to counterfeit. When Duchamp said, "Art is whatever I say it is," he was telling the truth. When Andy Warhol says it, he's putting us on. Other artists may sometimes take a while to come around to a new, true form, as when Picasso was at first indignant at Lipchitz' use of paint on his sculptures and then two weeks later described the technique as a great discovery; but true artists do come around to true art eventually, becuase that is what the artist is: the one who knows art when he sees it.

Unfortunately, one can expect no precision—not even much agreement—in these matters, since the man who really knows cannot prove he knows. William Blake swore Joshua Reynolds was in the service of the devil, and it was true, though Reynolds got all the commissions. Brahms loved the waltzes of Strauss; snobs and fakes were aghast—and are still. Since bad art has a harmful effect on society, it should never go un-challenged; but since the bad artist (like the good one) is an artist at all only because he claims he is, and has gotten at least one other person to believe him, how is he to be challenged? The only available rules are those of the gunfighter.

Artists have been shooting at artists for centuries. It's a healthy sport if managed with a measure of civility, gun against gun, nothing personal or mean. Being forced to articulate and defend a position can make a bad artist better—people are more educable than we generally admit—and a stupid defense, though not always proof that the art is fraudulent, can alert people to the strong possibility that the artist is a fool, or emo-tionally cracked, or a philistine in cunning disguise. In any case, a little loud shouting between artists about art can bring the community back into the debate and thus, besides improving business, protect the world from arrogant pretenders who claim to be above mere mortal explanation—the Nietzsches of the arts, who think it the business of ordinary clods to blink, shut their mouths, and try to follow.

The gunfighting of artists is already common, of course. The fiercest and most interesting book reviews in the *New York Times* are by writers. My object here is therefore not to start up such gunfighting, or even to encourage it, but to make it a little more or-derly, a little more deadly.

Art does not work rationally, not even the art of liter-ature—though literary people are forever congratu-lating themselves on the fact that, unlike painters, sculptors, and musicians, they still know what's up. They hear of Bruce Conners finding a doll in a city dump and placing it in a moldering high chair, then moving it to a museum, where it is celebrated (in this case rightly) as a work of art, and they cry, delighted, that you can't get away with a thing like that in literature. Or they listen to music constructed out of electronic bleeps and street noises and they lean back comfortably, secure in their understanding that all this, though fools may enjoy it, is a sickness of the times. Literature cannot fall into such error because literature is language, and language is by nature a sane expression of consciousness. As a psychologist might put it, every remark from a sane man asserts that 1) a certain person is 2) communicating something 3) in some situation 4) to someone. Deny any one of these terms (let the speaker assert that he is not himself but Jesus Christ, or let him speak gibberish, or let him insist that the hospital is an airbase or that the person he addresses is Napoleon) and you have psychotic speech. The difference between true art and false, the smug maintain, is that true art is rational. Even superficially, the definition of psychotic speech ought to frighten the smug. The novelist always claims he's someone else, denies that communication is his purpose (often speaking what to the general reader seems gibberish), and makes up out of his own head both situation and audience.

"Art tells the truth," Chekhov says; according to Tolstoy, art tells the truth because it "expresses the highest feelings of man." These may well be two statements of the same thing, but whether they are or not, what do they mean? How do we apply them? A group of people from all over the world, all of whom describe themselves as artists and therefore may be, converge in Paris to chop apart an automobile and spread wet spaghetti on a woman who has taken all her clothes off. Is it true? What is the nature of the lofty feeling? Is this alleged happening less true, the feeling less lofty, than what we get out of the nearly impenetrable odes of Pindar, the comic quotation of the *William Tell* Overture in Shostakovich's *Symphony* no. 15, the stern Christianity of *Njal's Saga* or *Gulliver's Travels,* or the godless terror of John Hawkes' *The Beetleleg?*

The meaning of art is hard to define satisfactorily, as we've seen. If I want you to know what my childhood was like, I tell you stories—how my father used to go up and down our country road in the middle of winter on his wired-together Farmall tractor, plowing out our neighbors' driveways, getting no pay but talk and hot coffee; how my mother taught English to people who didn't like it much and how she retreated at last to teaching third grade; how she read aloud to my father when he milked the cows and sang harmony with him on *The Old Rugged Cross;* and how (let us say I'm so stupid as to say) all of us were intense and happy and more or less afraid of the dark. If you are a sociologist or philosopher or a representative of the government, you can reduce all this by analysis to a socio-economic description; in other words, a different kind of understanding. When you have done this as well as it can be done, I will say, perhaps irritably, that you've missed the whole point. If you patiently ask, Then what *was* the point? I tell more stories or retire in a funk.

Granting for the moment that the artist cannot say in strictly logical or mathematical language exactly what he means, let us go on to ask how he says whatever it is he says: how are some stories more true—that is, valid—than others? As you know, the picture of my childhood that I've just set down is a lie. I don't mean that it's fiction—it's more or less true as far as it goes— but that it's a distortion. To take the most obvious detail, the phrase "all of us were intense and happy and more or less afraid of the dark" is sentimental tripe, despite the clownish labor of the "more or less." It *feels* sentimental, downright creepy in fact. (Bad art is always basically creepy; that is its first and most obvious identifying sign. Warhol. Philip Roth. The fellow who shoots himself, if he's still with us.) Saying the thing in the wrong way calls up wrong associations. The statement needs revision and a realized context, something that will rule out the sentimental cheapness—in other words, it needs, among other things, stories that will nail it down. It may be that I cannot make my meaning plain except by making up some situation that never really happened. It may be that I can only be plain by speaking as though I were a fool and thus forcing the reader to back off from me to where I want him (Chaucer's way). It may be that I can sneak up on my meaning by abandoning language altogether and howling at the reader in what would be called—in this case mistakenly—gibberish.

Whatever the method I end up choosing, and whether I "communicate" something true (my childhood) or something wholly made up (the childhood of Godzilla), it works or not depending on how it feels. This does not mean that all one feels uneasy about should be abandoned. Perfectly comfortable art is dead art, the product of an embalmed mind that has nothing to say to anyone, even the aesthetically dead. One is frequently uncomfortable telling the truth in a new way or for the first time. It's like saying with conviction that one has seen the Loch Ness monster when in fact one has. But there's a difference between the statement that feels disquieting—the statement that makes one feel "weird," mysteriously vulnerable—and the statement that simply feels creepy.

Making weird statements that one feels to be true and then trying to make them stick is art's way of coming to understanding. Or, to put it another way, though the artist may have a clear impression, he doesn't know until he finishes speaking exactly what it is that he will be forced to say.

Everyone has had the experience of listening to and struggling to take part in an argument in which somehow the truth keeps eluding its hunters. One sits nervously on edge, wide awake, sensing with every nerve end the truth that will not show itself, trying to put one's finger on where the speakers are going wrong, and at last, if one is lucky, recognizing, with a shock of relief, what it is that needs to be stated. No one who has had the experience will deny that he knew all along that the elusive truth was there; he knew the truth "intuitively," we say. In the Platonic metaphor (or anyway one likes to think it was a metaphor) he "remembered" it but remembered it indistinctly. He could not *know* what he knew until he found words for it. My example doesn't apply merely to intellectuals. People who talk about raising chickens, people who are unfairly accused of things they are almost but not quite guilty of, and people trying to show how they felt about that fellow with the beard in Florida have all been through the same thing. All understanding is an articulation of intuitions.

One way of saying what the artist's intuition is, is saying what it's not. Like the philosopher, the scientist, and the preacher, the artist bangs for the world's attention and declares with gusto and conviction, *It's like this.* Since Aristotle won and Plato lost, "philosopher" here means the analytical philosopher: a man whose intuition is that the world is, from end to end, structured. He may declare that he knows the key to the scheme and may then, in Whitehead's words (at the beginning of *Process and Reality*),

frame a coherent, logical, necessary system of general ideas in terms of which every element of our experience can be interpreted. . . . By this notion of "interpretation" I mean that everything of which we are conscious, as enjoyed, perceived, willed, or thought, shall have the character of a particular instance of the general scheme. Thus the philosophical scheme should be coherent, logical, and, in respect to its interpretation, applicable and adequate. Here "applicable" means that some items of experience are thus interpretable, and "adequate" means that there are no items incapable of such interpretation.

Whitehead is describing the process of philosophical inquiry from Aristotle up to but not including Wittgenstein: the process of system spinning. Most contemporary philosophy reflects a revolution in philosophical method and expectation, but no change in the fundamental loyalty of the good philosophical mind. Some things are "inexpressible": one can know the definition of a red fire truck, and one ought to; one cannot know about total reality, one can only arrive at angles of vision, ways of trying to know. Broadly and inaccurately, for the old-time speculative philosopher reality is truth; for the contemporary philosopher you can't get there from here. Trivial modern philosophers leap to the mistaken notion that truth is not there, but this is a confusion of method and subject: it is true that the subject of philosophy is philosophical technique, but the purpose of the technique, whether this purpose is remembered or not, is to chase an intuition. For most modern philosophers, that grand old image of *logos*, the sun, has degenerated to a light bulb in a roomful of men born blind. The light is still on, the blind men assert with blind men's faith and disinterested pleasure, but they do not ask of one another such senseless questions as "What does it look like?" and "Is it friendly?" The philosopher's hunt for his intuition has, by and large, broken down; the horses have died, and the dogs are away chasing field mice. It is significant that those who still fight to continue the old, high pursuits—Paul Weiss, Roman Ingarden, Justus Buchler, for example—

are virtually unreadable, their thought borne up by an outrageous, utterly exhausting labor of language.

The scientist, too, has a feeling that the world is systematic; what he loves, however, is not the total scheme of relationships but the mechanical connections. Reality, for him, is a system of formulas which come together, hopefully, in some super-formula, perhaps the quantum theory. Science, like philosophy, has suffered some troublesome reversals of late. The laws of thermodynamics don't work if you're small enough or large enough to slip past them. And that's the least of it. What is an honest man to do in a universe where cause need not always preceed effect or have any observable relationship in space? But science plunges on heroically, hunting for the wires that have got to be there, exposing the Great Magician's tricks; and philosophers, artists, and men of religion smile hopefully and give the scientist foolish suggestions.

The reality-hunter most like the artist is the man of religion—the man whose primary intuition is that the world is holy. Like the artist, he does not articulate his intuition by analyzing his way to a proof that what he guessed all along was right; instead, he tells a story. Reality, he says thoughtfully, is like this . . . and he makes up the story of Job, or of the dying Buddha, or of Achilles. As the figure of the poet-priest found in every old society makes clear, it is impossible to distinguish between the primitive artist and the primitive holy man. Cows and horses were the same thing in the days of the Devonian fish. If they differ now, it is because they have adapted to different functions. When a critic takes the story of a poet-priest, analyzes it and interprets it and insists that every word is literally true, a matter of doctrine and history, never to be altered, the poet-priest is reduced to a priest, and the critic is a theologian. If the critic, on the other hand, interprets the story as metaphoric expression of a philosophical idea, the poet-priest is made a poet. In their essence, in other words, the idea of holiness and the idea of beauty are one and the same. God, after all, is merely a word which the poet-priest uses to express a synthesis of feelings he cannot express otherwise except by telling stories, some of which are "true" (things he saw happen or heard about), some of which are fables.

To recognize the identity of beauty and holiness is to get rid of a confusion which has plagued aestheticians for centuries. *Beauty* is an apparently meaningless word which we continue to use because we understand it. Beauty is something that doesn't exist except in the instant it jars the soul and thus at once comes into being and attracts. Beauty is something that happens in life, but confusedly and unpredictably, and something that happens, infallibly, in true art. It is something that "gets across"—that is, makes profound but finally inexpressible sense, as Tillich says, "on the level of deep experience," whatever that means.

Let me try to make this less vague.

The primary intuition of the poet-priest is one of a particular sort of order, an order which is partly sensuous, made up of objects loved or hated, partly transcendent and abstract, a vague but powerful sense of the general classes of things which *ought* to be loved or hated; in other words, affirmed or blown to bits. What he loves the artist calls beautiful; what he hates he has no word for (not "ugly," or "grotesque," or "trivial," or "wicked"), he merely wants it *out*. He cannot get it out, of course. The best he can do is get it clear, know where the beautiful—all that is metaphorically summed up by the word *life*—connects with the not-beautiful; that is, with *death*. "Up" against "down," "light" against "dark." The artist who, like Samuel Beckett, claims the two are the same thing—so that the age-old intuition of the artist is a lie, just one more stupid illusion, and who therefore turns on all we have found "so wonderful!" and smoothes it over with sand—is in the same room as the blind philosopher, a room many artists of the present age find it hard to break out of. Yet as Beckett knows ("Where are you going?" "On.") the artist is not quite in the philosopher's predicament. It is impossible for art *not* to assert man's intuition of the beautiful, whether the artist knows this is so or not. It either asserts or it stops being art. Insofar as the long dead "Art Is Dead" movement felt like art, it denied its nihilistic premise. If it meant to offer an Aristotelian imitation of actual process (reality as pointless destruction), it failed in supremely Hegelian fashion: we deny, though perhaps with misgivings, that the artist has told the whole truth; we affirm, as perhaps he too does in secret, though he lies to himself, that second half of the half-truth told by the artist. In the act of flinching from the nihilist's assertion, we make our opposing affirmation.

All this is to say that the artist can approach the beautiful in a thousand ways—by trying to imitate it straight, by painting its monstrous opposite, or in any of the ways in between. As priest he tells what God loves and hates; as poet he drops the divine metaphor and stands himself as lawgiver. His fundamental sense, as he looks at life, is of glory obstructed: a glimpsed wholeness shattered. What gets in his way may lie outside him: a foolish and wrongheaded society, a vast spider web of maliciously misleading doctrine, or what seems to him an overwhelming tradition of artistic error, a tradition which has come to be barren and empty of what it was made to give life to. Or what gets in his way may lie *inside* him: the infuriating limitations of his own technique and mind, the fact that eventually he must die. In one case the artist's response may be to fight with all his heart the society, the doctrine, or the tradition which would kill him; in the other case, he does his ultimately inadequate best. He may consciously and systematically rebuild his technique, even his mind—may go so far as to drive himself insane, ceasing to be an artist, by burning himself in the zealot's fires of heroin or politics or sex. He may turn himself into a monstrously conscious and deadly imitation of the psychotic rapist or killer.

The passion of true art involves risks, one may as well admit. Like philosophers, scientists, and men of religion, even sane artists can outreach their society's capacity for understanding and become, for that society, intolerable. On the one hand, they are the spokesmen of a reality man cannot live without, whatever people may foolishly imagine; on the other hand, their zeal for a certain kind of truth can reach flat opposition to the civilization that has nourished them. The artist who, like Jean-Jacques Lebel, believes that art and society have come to "la guerre totale," understands that if he loses the war he will die. Nevertheless, the revolutionary artist has a great advantage over the society which, if he is right, stands like a high-pocketed pig surveying its ladies magazines and decorator lamps and Styrofoam chairs, unaware of the butcher on the landing. Yet the pig is better off than he deserves to be. Under the bed, with cunning eyes, machine-gun trained on the door, there is another artist to protect him. One of these artists must surely be wrong. How do we know which?

The sense of the beautiful or holy, which the artist and the man of religion share as their main obsession, has often been described—most eloquently by Immanuel Kant—as "independent of all interest." One must, according to this point of view, avoid confusing the beautiful with the *agreeable,* on the one hand, and the *good,* on the other. The agreeable, Kant says, is what gratifies a man; the beautiful is what pleases him; and the good is what man approves. To a grower of oranges, a picture of an orange grove is agreeable; he is hardly indifferent to whether or not real orange groves exist in the world. To a dying old lady, a picture of Christ emerging from the tomb is both agreeable and good: she is gratified that such things can happen, and she approves of the thought that something of the same sort may happen to her.

Since Kant is dead and cannot defend himself, let us raise questions. Say I have an orange grove, and say that I like art. What am I really looking at when I look at a picture of an orange grove? One possibility can be dismissed at once: I am *not* looking at an orange grove but at a picture; in other words, an opinion of orange groves, or anyway of one orange grove. As an orange-grove specialist myself, I have my own opinion, which, because I like art, I am trying to fit with the opinion of the artist. The oranges, I observe, are oranger than I would have expected. "Curious!" I muse. Perhaps I add, "It's true!" In this case I am looking at what I take to be the artist's *message,* which I accept or reject. But if this is so, what I am really looking at is the indifferent question, How orange is an orange? I do not care what the answer is any more than I care how much seven and six adds up to; I merely want to know the right answer.

Now suppose the artist is a clever one whose oranges, as I fixedly stare at them, are sometime sensibly orange and sometimes blue. "Curious!" I muse again, and I began to distrust the oranges in my grove. What am I looking at now—the real nature of oranges, or technique, or both? Or am I looking perhaps at something larger, other experiences which shift in this same way? I am now, of course, reading a different message: things change. Or I am looking at a different indifferent question, To what extent is that thing stable? And I am satisfied with the ridiculous answer, That's a very interesting question. I am lying, of course. A question is only interesting while you think about it. But I have been driven to think about it, if only for a moment, and I am amused.

Now suppose the artist, who has the heart of a devil, says "Good!" and substitutes a different picture, one which, to infuriate me, he has meticulously copied (I know only by the card he tacks to the wall) from an ancient Burmese representation of an orange grove. Burmese monks, I for some reason happen to know, made a fetish of keeping all sign of the individual artist out of the picture. What am I to say? I could say that the new message is pure technique: the perfection of the copy. But I am leery now, I anticipate the artist's next move—the same picture carelessly done in feces and human hair. What I say therefore is, "Fraud!" But I do not really feel sure of myself. He is the artist, after all, and he tells me, with apparent sincerity, that it's art, or at least an attempt. He says he'll stake his life on it. "It's hanging in a museum, isn't it?" he says hopefully. We purse our lips, artist and viewer, and reflect. We glance at the museum director. He shrugs. "It's a business, Mac. Art is what people come look at to see if it's art."

All this is very discouraging, at first. But the museum director is smarter than he looks. When people stop coming to see if what is hanging on the walls is art, the reason will be that it is not. Either it never was art in the first place, or else it was and has stopped being. Patiently returning time after time, like believers to the cave of a dead oracle, and learning that nothing will happen there, they have quit. There is no more art, or in any event, no more art in museums. If this is so, beauty is a generalized human feeling (purity of heart) which is brought to focus and released by the art object, a thing as indifferent to beauty, in itself, as a radio tube is indifferent to the music of Schubert. Beauty in art, in other words, is the same thing as beauty in life: it happens in connection with certain objects and events, only in art it happens regularly, through the conscious agency of some artist, if only because it is expected. Art, like an addict's needle, is an instrument.

No one will be satisfied with that definition, or should be; but it brings us this far: we can answer Kant by saying that in our experience of the beautiful, the agreeableness or disagreeableness of the representation is a matter of chance, a variable of no significance. It may be that in looking at a picture of a nude we find gratification interfering with the aesthetic experience, as it does when adolescents look at half-naked ladies by old masters; but it is also possible that gratification may, in a given work, be itself the aesthetic experience or its trigger. It may even be, in a particular work, that frustration is the aesthetic experience. This is art, we are told. We stare and stare, desperately hoping for some holy sign, but no sign comes. The desperate hope is the affirmation; the museum and the work are a shockingly expensive and cruel trick designed to make the affirmation rise. Not that this is a fair explanation of all contemporary nonsense art. And I do not mean either that all frustrating art is equally good, equally important. There are as many kinds of frustration, moreover, as there are kinds of human affirmation. It is one thing to be infuriated by a huge, square, uncut block of steel, another to be consternated by a stuffed ram with a tire around it. Neither frustration has anything to do with that which comes from looking at a dead human hand with an ornamental hat pin sticking through it. Before such monstrosities criticism flies. How can one say that they are good or not good? Yet one does. One can blindly intuit what the artist feels, and one can cry out—if only to see if it is true—"You fool! *Fool!* The *pin* should be longer!"

Art, we reply to Kant, sneaking along with fear and trembling (puns are fair), is not independent of all interest but beyond all interest. It is an affirmation of what ought to be and what, in the artist's devout opinion, *is*, whether or not it can be reached from where we are. For a grave-digger it is agreeable to see Antigone go out and bury her dead; for Nietzsche it is worthy of approval as a triumph of moral feeling over the merely social feeling of Creon. But neither the grave-digger nor Nietzsche looks at Sophocles' play with mere interest: they affirm, as feeling creatures, that even if there were no profession of digging graves, no possible recurrence of Antigone's problem, the dead should be buried; the dignity of life demands it. And even if science can overcome the inconvenience of death, and human beings can live forever, the play will be moving at least when understood in its historical context. It affirms an absolute one cannot turn one's back on, a beauty of feeling embodied in the life of a woman who stands as the figure of every woman's potential, every human being's potential, even a grave-digger's, even Nietzsche's.

I have obviously not said what kind of intuition is peculiar to the artist, though I have tried to creep up on it with stories; and I have not said what makes a twentieth-century artist different from a twentieth-century priest. These questions cannot be dropped because they help to explain the kind of articulation of the original intuition which proves satisfying to an artist.

The primary intuition of an artist, then, is that what is best in life, which he extends to mean what is best in all the universe, is "the level of deep experience." *His* experience, he means. Not the deepest experience of a philosopher (primarily an intellectual experience), but that of a man who, by chemistry, is doomed to be an artist. If philosophers are deeply moved by art it is because they are also partly, but not primarily, tuned in to the roar of beauty. The idea of beauty informs the experience of all human beings: some merely dip their toes in it, some wade out in it—as Alexander went out into the ocean to be thought a god—and drown. The artist's affirmation, or, more precisely, his search for affirmation, is the work of art. Thus all works of art are affirmations of the same thing: they differ from one another because they are different ways of trying to make the age-old affirmation, because every artist's mind and every age throws up its own impediments to affirmation, and because, finally, not all affirmations are equally intense or broad—in other words, not all artists are to the same degree or in the same way obsessed. The form that art takes, the quality of the artist's mind and civilization, and the intensity of diverse affirmations all fall on a scale which runs from *slight* to *overwhelming,* or from the "beautiful" to the "sublime."

I need not spell out all the implications of this statement. Let me jump to the fact that correct assessment of the pressure of an artist's affirmation cannot safely treat the work of art in isolation from its background: the tradition behind the work and the moment (time and place) of its appearance. A soap carving is one thing on a mantelpiece and another in a museum, one thing if its obvious purpose is to be a lovely trifle (a soap carving), another if it seems to stand as a cynical joke (a soap carving usurping the place of a statue carved out of granite). I am speaking now only of good soap carvings and good granite statues—works in which technique is adequate to purpose. (The artist who works at what he's trying to say so clumsily that he cannot get it said, and the artist whose statement is so much like everybody else's that nobody finds it worth listening to—these are frauds, apprentices, or fools.)

The most obvious manifestation of the scale from slight to overwhelming is the continuum which runs between those old misnamed categories, the beautiful and the sublime. If the beautiful is, as Edmund Burke said, the small, the curvalinear, smooth, and so forth, while the sublime is huge and angular and rough, then what Burke ought to have meant by the beautiful is the pleasant, comfortable, and relatively trifling affirmation (an ethical one, in Kierkegaard's terminology), and by the sublime he should have meant hard-won, defiant affirmations (moral). The first celebrates what can be domesticated and enjoyed, what makes life pleasant or can anyway be tolerated: a bowl of roses, a stuffed ram which, like us, is somehow obstructed and out of place, stuck inside a tire, but is willing, barely, to put up with the joke. The sublime, on the other hand, celebrates mankind's defiance—like Thor's—of the awesome powers which will one of these days destroy him: mad Lear fending off the powers of evil, or art's shrewd crackpots chopping up a car in Paris and spreading spaghetti on a naked girl. *Lear* and the Paris happening have only their *kind* of affirmation in common. Insofar as the two "works" are effective, the observer violently asserts himself against man's extinction by brainless Fate or the brainless mechanization of modern life.

Though they were once the same thing (the poet-priest), the artist and priest are now, as we've said, two different things. How the original separation came about is as follows. There was once a wise old poet-priest who had two sons, to whom he taught all his stories, all his dances, and all his magic. Each son was extremely bright in certain ways but in other ways stupid. The elder (it is sometimes mistakenly reported that he was the younger) was a literal-minded, intensely loyal person who believed all the stories and tried to live by them. They were helpful, for the most part, but sometimes they failed him. He worried about this and sometimes thought he would go out of his mind, and sometimes did, but then he discovered that he too could make up stories, really further elaborations of principles he'd learned from his father's stories without knowing it. He found, too, that sometimes new stories told by strangers illuminated dark places in his father's stories. He married an intelligent, literal-minded girl (the first analytic philosopher), and soon they had a son, who, at the age of twelve, became the first theologian. This son in turn interpreted *his* father's stories and made of their principles a set of laws. From then on all the people lived happily and confidently except now and then when something turned up suggesting that the original poet-priest's stories were a pack of lies.

As for the younger of the two sons of the first poet-priest, he listened to his father's stories with extreme care and turned them over and over in his mind, not so much because they were useful or true (he supposed they must be more or less true, one way or another) as because they reminded him of everything he liked and made his feelings about things clearer to him. As he grew older he began to have feelings not covered by his father's stories. For one thing, he felt vaguely resentful of his older brother, who had risen to a position of power in the community and had vast herds of sheep and was married to a girl the younger brother blindly, foolishly loved. For another thing, he hated the way his brother and his followers told the old man's stories: they missed the point. He grew even more angry when his brother's son began turning the stories into laws, especially since one of the laws was that everybody had to work because work was "beloved of the gods." The original poet-priest's younger son was a lazy oaf, if the truth be told. He grudgingly took up raising corn and, walking back and forth behind his ox, he played out in his mind little fantasies of what he would do if he ever got his brother's wife alone or found his brother walking in the woods in the middle of the night. Eventually, of course, it all came to pass. He found himself alone with his sister-in-law, and being too timid to seduce her he made up what amounted to a story on the subject of how he felt about her. She was more impressed than he could have dared hope, and when they met again she subtly led him into telling her certain parts of it again, with more feeling. One night her husband caught them together, and at a sign from the woman—a sign she did not know she gave—the younger brother slew the elder. They buried him, and as they were tamping down the dirt a voice yelled at them out of heaven, "Cain! Where's your brother?" They fled, naturally, and before long they had a son who listened eagerly to his father's stories. He had his father's indifference to their literal truth, his mother's penchant for analysis, and so, at the age of thirty-two or -three he became the world's first literary critic.

Whether or not this little history is true, it is clear that art and religion are now two separate things, even though the artist speaks of "holiness" like a preacher and preachers speak shamelessly of "beauty." And it is clear, though it may not be readily admitted, that artists are people who seek to understand through art, while preachers seek to understand by preaching. (A preacher knows more about religion when he finishes preaching a careful sermon than he did when he sat down to write it.) The articulation which satisfies an artist is directly analogous to that which satisfies a preacher: an interpretation of the experience of his own time and place, summed up in the person of the artist or preacher, developed through the medium of the whole tradition of, in one case, art, and in the other case, doctrine. The work produced by a mentally or emotionally limited artist is called bad art. The work produced by a mentally or emotionally limited preacher is called bad religion or heresy.

To speak of "tradition and individual talent" is to speak misleadingly, though not incorrectly. We would do better to speak of the convergence of tradition and the individual artist's moment. The artist is a man of maximum sensitivity, a man who sees and feels more things in more precise detail than do the people around him, partly because he has excellent emotional and intellectual equipment, including—above all, perhaps—the security which makes for shamelessness, and partly because he has special machinery for seeing and feeling: the tradition of his art. The man whose sense of beauty is most easily triggered by visual things can learn, if he wants to, the tricks of vision worked out by painters, sculptors, and the like from before the dawn of recorded history; a good musician can listen to the music of his time with the whole tradition of music in his head, not only Eastern and Western music but African and South American Indian as well. The man who understands by means of words has at hand, if he wants it, nearly all human language.

If tradition and individual talent, understood in the usual sense, were the relevant machinery, art would be better today than it has ever been before: we have not only our own great traditions but also those of cultures that used to be closed off—for example, Tibet—and we have talented artists. The artist does not extend his tradition by the force of his own personality or talent. Mechanical as a pipe fitter, he tries to find a way to fit his own experience (in other words, the feelings of his time and place) to the tradition of his art. To put this still another way, the *medium* of any given art is everything that has ever been done in it, or everything the artist is aware of in his tradition. The medium for the first sculptor may have been mud, but the second sculptor worked with a more complex substance: mud and his experience of the first sculptor's work.

Just now especially, the past and its art seem to comment bitterly on the present. Artists who come back from fighting modern wars find it difficult to speak with conviction of the gallantry and heroism of soldiering. Artists involved with the vast bureaucratic pork barrel called higher education are inclined to speak little of the beauty of wisdom. Feelings of skepticism about traditional values are the dominant feelings of the age, feelings the artist must find his way over or around or under if he's to make the affirmation which defines him. Even if some of these feelings are wrong, mere mistaken emotion—like the feeling of a lover who thinks he hears his lady coming, but it's only the mailman not bringing any mail—they are the driving emotions of men and women with whom the artist is involved and for whom he cannot help but feel a sympathy which ends up confusing him. They are the artist's only available subject. They are what he must paint or make music of. Somehow he must find a way to make people who deny that they are heroes, who may even insist that they are buckets of worms, fit as if naturally into novelistic situations designed for people who considered themselves heroes. What happens in art is that neither tradition nor the artist's own moment comes off unchanged. Tradition is stretched to make room for what it never meant to swallow, and the moment is forced to admit its relationship with the dead. Of course the less the artist knows about tradition—the greater his ignorance or stupidity—the greater the power of the moment, the less the intellectual and emotional testing of present fancy against all that has gone before. This is one of the reasons so much art today is bad. If he's not well-educated, wise, and careful, the artist who loves beauty and cannot find it in the world around him may give up the attempt to reaffirm, to raise nobility from the dead, and may satisfy himself with mere expression of his own disappointment, pain, and anger.

An artist is someone who believes in art, who believes that art reflects something which is real in life, who tries to see and reveal to others what life is in his own time by making it art. If he panders to his time, saying what his time says no matter how his art cries out against him, he is a witch, and dangerous: Tennyson, for instance, in his praise—or seeming praise—of what happened at the valley of death. If he panders to tradition, paying no mind to the howls and whimpers and giggles of his age, he is a self-righteous pedant and nostalgia-monger, an impediment to civilized progress.

What kind of articulation of his intuition satisfies the artist? The answer is, one which honestly feels to him like art and which people he tentatively trusts are willing to look at to see if it is art. Insofar as the artist's purpose is complex, not expression of a feeling so simple that a bold metaphor will do (a huge letter *H* made of railroad spikes welded to sheet metal) but expression of, say, his love for his children or his unpluralistic belief that one kind of life is better than another, the artist cannot predict in advance what form his work will ultimately take. Some novels are written for experiment's sake, but these are rarely novels worth reading. The true experimental novel, like Biely's *Petersburg,* or Beckett's *Malone Dies,* is one which achieves the form it does because it cannot otherwise say what is to be said.

When the artist has moved as far from the tradition of the novel as either of these novels has moved, he has nothing to guide him but his feeling as he writes, and again and again as he rereads his work, that it is still art; it still triggers in him the feeling that art triggers. He calls in the reader. The reader looks as honestly and carefully as he can (let us wishfully think), and in the end he says, "It's good," or else, "It stinks." If the latter, the reason may be that the work does stink. Or it may be, the artist knows, that criticism is getting in the reader's way: he is looking wrong. Or it may be that perverse social values are getting in the way—the reader does not appreciate the values the artist has recorded or celebrated and is not sufficiently disgusted by what ought to disgust him in the world. It may be, too, that the artist has simply jumped too far and cannot be rightly understood until a century or so has passed—Blake, for instance. But finally, it does not matter to the artist what judgment the viewer comes to *as long as he looks.* The man who blows up grand pianos is howled at from every side, "Fraud! Not art!" but what counts is that the crowd is there to howl, though it may not be there next time. Something happens to them as they watch the instrument blown up—some will even admit it. They experience a shock of terrible metaphor—"Grand pianos are in my way, the whole tradition is in my way, and *you* are in my way: I can say nothing, do nothing, affirm nothing because of the piano's intolerable high-tone creamy plinking, which you fools adore; I will therefore destroy them, I will destroy you all!" (Whether the destroyer is a sculptor, a musician, or a confidence man is somewhat difficult, in this case, to make out.) In a curiously similar way, marauding war-kings were in Homer's way. With the dynamite of epic tradition, developed in the first place to celebrate their names, he blew them to smithereens.

Not, again, that a dynamited piano equals *The Iliad.* You have to see a piano blown up to really get the metaphor, and the repeatability of the experience is somewhat limited by practical considerations. Besides, instantaneous metaphor, even if it manages not to be stupid—as this piano one is—is neither as clear nor as significant as the systematically extended metaphor of fable or musical composition.

I have still not gotten to the question, What makes some good art great and worth fighting over? Or, if all good art is an honest attempt, direct or indirect, at beauty-affirmation, why is only some art worth preserving? The intensity of the affirmation itself is obviously not enough to explain this. No one was ever as shaken to the bowels by anything in *The Iliad* as we are by the pure violence of seeing an artist allow himself to be shot, yet the experience of *The Iliad* has infinitely greater staying power. What counts is not the pressure but the inclusiveness and total energy of the artist's affirmation. Great art, like great philosophy, is metaphysical—but emotionally metaphysical. To paraphrase the passage I quoted from Whitehead earlier, *it frames a coherent, convincing, necessary system of general ideas and feelings in terms of which every element of our experience is illuminated.* The advantage of all arts over philosophy, as Croce understood, is that the metaphysics of art cannot break down. A logical system falls the moment any element of its logic is proved to be either wrong or arbitrary. An emotional system remains valid as long as people continue to feel that it is valid; that is, as long as when you prick them they bleed. It is true that we have learned in the past century that men's sensitivities can be changed or destroyed: men can be changed into monsters, as they were in Nazi Germany, or they can be indoctrinated by the subtle force of their society into conceiving themselves to be devoid of free will, as many people have been in the United States. It can be shown by infallible or at least official logic that values are all a matter of opinion, that what seems good in one culture (like eating babies to improve one's virility) seems unpleasant to another. It can be proved positively that everything is relative. But not to an artist.

By the nature of the case, the rightness of the artist is beyond demonstration, though there are curious evidences that it is sometimes real. If art is relative, a cultural matter, we should expect that people of one culture would be unresponsive to the best art of another, and indeed anthropologists have shown that they are. The music of Beethoven is obscene to most black Africans: bloated, disgustingly over-rich, and rhythmically simplistic. Japanese Buddhist art, similarly, seems unimaginative and trifling to most Americans. But with *artists* of diverse cultures this seems not to hold. When samples of mixed good and bad art from one culture are shown or performed for the artists of another, the artists of the second culture seem to be able to distinguish good from bad. Fascinating work on this has been done by, among others, Adrien Gerbrands of the Leyden Museum in Leyden, Netherlands. Playing European music for illiterate and untraveled but highly professional black African musicians, Gerbrands discovered that the Africans' judgments are surprisingly close to those that are for us musical history.

Whatever value we may wish to place on such evidence, the fact remains that in culture after culture artists have proclaimed repeatedly that art in some sense "tells the truth." Show the artist a Nazi Frankenstein monster and his reaction is simple—"Get it out!" Why one should get the monster out the artist may not exactly know, at least insofar as he speaks as an artist. The monster is an impediment, an error: he obstructs the path to beauty. The gods, Plato would say, have whispered in the artist's ear.

Art, in short, asserts an ultimate rightness of things which it does not pretend to understand in the philosopher's way but which it nevertheless can understand and show mankind. There are degrees of this showing. The artist who celebrates the trivial and tame—a pleasant sunset, a good Christmas dinner—reinforces what is trivially good in his society. He is brother to the artist who attacks what is trivially evil in his time: the comic poet, the satirist, the writer of musical jokes. A higher (but still not very high) kind of artist adopts the stance of his time and toys with it, suggesting indirectly the existence of something better, something truer. The contemporary chance composer is an example. He takes the prevailing notion of his time, that all life is a matter of chance (an idea which reduces the mind to mere substance), and he makes what he calls music of it. We listen to four radios, arbitrarily tuned, and to three or four musicians who, without consulting one another, struggle with their violins and horns and balloons to make sense of the chance noise. If the clued-in audience feels that some kind of sense is indeed emerging, even a new order of sensation, it has climbed above its normal, debased notion of man; if the audience hears only tiresome noise, it has at least the affirmation of its anger. The great artist, whatever the form he chooses, breaks through the limited reality around him and makes a new one. He says not "It surely can't be just this!" but "Listen, it's like this!" And makes it stick.

Every fair-minded person will readily admit that not all bad or mediocre artists should be dismissed from our republic. There is a place for the amusing poem, the John Cage joke (though God knows it wears thin), the Rauschenberg ram (which does not). A place exists for chance composition just as for jazz, which it brainlessly burlesques: a place for blown-up pianos. The place for such art, admittedly, is now—not all time. It will pass, like a chicken dinner or a bad cold.

But while the fair-minded person makes room in his world for the trivial, the temporary, even the intentionally or accidentally fraudulent, such goodness is a luxury no artist can afford—certainly no young artist hunting a place to stand—and no critic who cares about true art will tolerate. Wherever it appears, from the drivel of politicians to moronic styles of dress, from television chaff-art to the stentorian fraudulence of "innovative fiction" at its worst, the bad is an obstruction of the light, a competitor against good, a filth and a pestilence that must be driven out. Every chance composition purposely or accidentally backs a lie. If the chance composer writes a book in which he explains himself, solemnly intoning that life is mere chance—for all the raging evidence of Hobbes, Spinoza, and Einstein—then he doubles the strength of his poison. Every nonsense artist, destructionist, or painter of bruised entrails on a field of burning red is a plague carrier, a usurper of space that belongs to the sons of God. For the poet, Yvor Winters says, poetry is "his finest mode of thinking and perceiving, of being, of discovering reality and participating in reality." It is his life, in short. Who can blame him if he lashes out in fury at those who would offer substitutes?

That is why, despite his pathetic wish to seem a gentleman, the true artist rants and rolls his eyes, or blinds and numbs himself with drink, or careens from woman to woman or man to man, or shuts himself away and refuses to see guests. Like an angel trapped in hell, he has dangerous eyes.

The poet-priest had two functions: lawgiver and comforter. He had to know what laws to give, what comfort to give, what comfort to withhold as false. The poet has far less power now, but the job hasn't changed. He must affirm, comfort as he can, and make it stick. Let artists say what they know, then, admitting the difficulties but speaking nonetheless. Let them scorn the idea of dismissing as harmless the irrelevant fatheads who steal museums and concert halls and library shelves: the whiners, the purveyors of high-tone soap opera, the calm accepters of senselessness, the murderers. It is not entirely clear that these people are not artists. They may be brilliant artists, with positions exactly as absolute as, say, mine. But they are wrong. It's not safe to let them be driven from the republic by policemen, politicians, or professional educators. Officialdom would drive out all of us, which is one reason that when we come out shooting we should all talk with dignity and restraint, like congressmen, and wear, like Doc Holliday, vests and ties. Let a state of total war be declared not between art and society—at least until society starts horning in—but between the age-old enemies, real and fake.

4

Art and Insanity

THROUGHOUT these chapters, I've been setting down a high-minded, if not downright stately picture of the artist. He's the conscious guardian of his society, the only man in town who's honest by profession. There's morality even in the process he works by; he may get cross, especially at inferior, dishonest artists, but it's all in a good cause. Such a picture, admittedly, does not jibe very well with the conventional notion that all true artists are crazy. That view of the artist is extremely common, not only in our culture but in many cultures, and though it may derive partly from the fact that art can at times be baffling (to many people, even the lyrics of the Beatles were, in the beginning, impenetrable), we know that there's surely more to the rumor that art inclines toward madness. Artists do on occasion behave oddly—living in sin, fighting with policemen, joining faraway minor revolutions, occasionally cutting off their ears. What is the truth about art and lunacy?

The chief quality that distinguishes great art, everyone knows, is its sanity, *the good sense and efficient energy with which it goes after what is really there and feels significant.*

Let me emphasize two main implications of this description. First, to say that something is "really there"—some right attitude or object of belief, or some situation whose existence challenges our too-easy certainties—is to assert a significant coherence in human experience: to assert that some beliefs and attitudes are beneficial for the flowering of sensation and consciousness, while others, to a greater or lesser degree, constrict and tend to kill. Great artists do regularly make this assertion. Thus Homer, through the character of Hector and Achilles, goes after a warrior-ideal of justice and self-sacrifice that is beyond the understanding of Priam and dog-eyed Agamemnon, at least when the poem opens—an ideal that gave Greek civilization its tone, and one without which Western civilization might not have flowered. Humanness is coherent and can go right or wrong; what's true for Hector and Achilles is true for all of us.

The second implication in need of emphasis is this: to say that artistic energy is "efficient" is to say that it does not spatter out in irrelevant directions, needlessly work against itself in futile self-contradiction, raising more doubt and difficulties than are warranted by the nature of the thing explored; and that it does not, on the other hand, make easy leaps, like careless mathematics which seeks right answers without understanding its means.

Energy does not in itself imply sanity. When we speak of the energy in a given work we mean, normally, the creative process which brought the work into being in the first place—the strenuous labor of thought and technique visible in the perfect control and authority of a Zen painting, on the one hand, or, on the other, in the completely *considered* quality, the massiveness and weight, of the opening lines of *Moby Dick*—a process repeated, more or less, in the consciousness of anyone who carefully and intelligently looks at the finished picture or reads the book. It is unimportant that occasionally a work's seeming energy is not a reflection of the creative process which brought it forth—as in the case of the accidental masterpiece which occurs when an artist looks at a painting he has left out in the rain and decides to keep it, rightly seeing in it a fine (albeit accidental) solution to the aesthetic problem he was working on before the storm. As a rule, achievement more directly reflects energy, is less a result of luck. Either way the effect is the usual effect of controlled energy; namely, power. A lovely, easily achieved piece of art can never be called great (even Mozart's genius and facility in the early works come unmoored beside his later works or the greatest works of Beethoven); and a work obsessively labored, tortuously constructed in pursuit of some trivial end is similarly unsatisfying (Edward MacDowell). In one we find too little energy. In the other, the considerable energy—the expenditure of time and hungry ambition (but insufficient intellect)—is not controlled.

"Controlled," we say; but the psychotic murderer has thoughts as sternly marshaled, as intense and electrical, as those of Socrates. Just how sane is that sanity which distinguishes great art? Was Blake not at least a trifle crazy, also Melville, Tolstoy, Gogol, Dickens, Proust, Gide, and Faulkner? To put it another way, is it true, as Plato thought, that the wonderful smiling sanity of Homer was a divine madness? Granted, insanity and divine madness are not really the same; but traditionally, for those who are for some reason attracted to the notion of the poet as lunatic, the distinction between the two has seemed petty. And in any event, poets—especially undistinguished poets—are forever comparing themselves to Cassandra, and everyone who has ever seriously attempted a long fiction knows how remarkably similar writing is, in some respects, to dreaming. The thinness of the line between genius and madness is an ancient cliché and definitely troublesome for the man out to argue that bad art does damage to society and the psyche while good art does good. Yet surely it is true that if we say that the artist's creative energy pursues something real—affirms some value which ought to be affirmed—then we cannot say in the same breath that art's value is a matter of opinion, that in these matters one man's meat is another's poison. We know how to respond when the question is put this way: taste is not open to dispute because it admits of no proofs, but there is nevertheless good taste and bad.

Moreover, the damage which can be done by bad art is demonstrable and has been verified repeatedly—the ways, that is, in which certain kinds of bad art can brutalize, enfeeble, confuse, or wrongfully support. *A Clockwork Orange* describes phenomena that exist: forcible alterations of behavior and even of consciousness. From the moral standpoint, bad art and good work by similar processes but have opposite effects, one supporting death and slavery, the other life and freedom; and the reason bad art can have any effect at all is that, although some things are indeed healthy and others poisonous, the truth of what is healthy can easily be subverted: some artists, and some people who respond to art, are like Mithridates or, at best, Rappuccini's daughter; either voluntarily or involuntarily they have become poison eaters, people cut off from what is normally healthy, so that they're bad people to eat supper or fall in love with.

The true artist's purpose, and the purpose of the true critic after him, is to show what is healthy, in other words *sane*, in human seeing, thinking, and feeling, and to point out what is not. He may point out what is central to the healthy function of the human spirit—he may deal with morals—in which case his work, if it is successful, is major; or he may point out what is healthy and unhealthy in relatively trivial situations—he may deal with morality as it is reflected in manners—in which case his work is minor. If the artist's statement of what ought to be and, at best, what is, is a statement the wise and healthy man cannot accept because he instantly sees through it, or *feels* through it—that is, he finds the so-called art "creepy"—then the artist's creative energy is misspent: it has gone after not what is there but something else, or has gone for the right thing but missed. We may admire the gusto in any case, but we distinguish between the gusto of Socrates and the gusto of Charles Manson.

One might leave it at that. People have forever been trying to describe the creative process, in particular the relationship of genius to madness, and when a conversation has been going a long time, and has finally died down, there's much to be said for leaving sleeping dogs lie, or burying dead horses, or whatever. Still, that business of poets endlessly claiming to be Cassandra is distinctly tiresome. It's hard to resist trying to get the distinctions between madness and artistic creation a little clearer.

One thing investigators of the psychology of creative people have demonstrated beyond doubt in the past thirty years is that creativity has something to do with obsession. The demons of Poe, Van Gogh, and Liszt are not exceptions but extreme cases of the rule. The tensions we find resolved or at least defined and dramatized in art are the objective release of tensions in the life of the artist. This shouldn't surprise us—indeed, it shouldn't make us bat an eye. It does not, in itself, make the artist very different from other productive men and women. This is not necessarily to say—as Freud seemed to say, though he may not have meant it—that art is sick; and certainly it is not to say, as Freud occasionally seemed to say, that the artist has no idea what he's doing. Art begins in a wound, an imperfection—a wound inherent in the nature of life itself—and is an attempt either to learn to live with the wound or to heal it. It is the pain of the wound which impels the artist to do his work, and it is the universality of woundedness in the human condition which makes the work of art significant as medicine or distraction.

What we mean by "wound" in this case of course is some wound to personality and self-confidence, something that attacks or threatens the dignity and self-respect of the artist and must be overcome if his personality is to be healthy. The wound may take any number of forms: doubt about one's parentage, fear that one is a fool or freak, the crippling effect of psychological trauma or the potentially crippling effect of alienation from the society in which one feels at home, whether or not any such society really exists outside the fantasy of the artist.

As this last example (alienation from one's home society) hints, the artist's vulnerability may be, as artists have for centuries insisted, that the artist is better than those around him, hence an annoyance or a threat. He is one who can see in the country of the blind. He pursues truth whether or not the pursuit is, in a given instance, useful or important; he will not settle for fashionable simplifications; he is forever raising silly objections, carping over small points, denying the obvious, defending the wicked, asking for precision where no precision is required.

This notion of the artist as better than other people is irritating, I admit. I remember how annoyed I was myself, as a young man, when I first came across it, I think in connection with pronouncements by and about Goethe, Proust, and Ezra Pound. I felt, I think rightly that the people I knew—my parents and friends—were as high-minded and decent as any poet. The poet's business, it seemed to me, is to celebrate or at least understand those people, not arrogantly raise himself above them, pompously proclaim himself the Romantic "great man" who imposes on the rest of poor miserable humanity the duty of groping through darkness, hunting out his footsteps. I would not now take that opinion back, but I might temper it a little. A thousand times since then I've been in conversations where no one seemed to care about the truth, where people argued merely to win, refused to listen or try to understand, threw in irrelevancies—some anecdote without conceivable bearing, some mere ego-flower. A thousand times I have heard some person—some casual acquaintance about whom I had no strong feeling—cruelly vilified, and have found that to rise in defense of mere fairness is to become, suddenly, the enemy. I have witnessed, repeatedly, university battles in which no one on any side would stoop to plain truth. I have seen, repeatedly, how positions which at first glance seem stirringly noble and idealistic—for example, the battle led by Cesar Chavez in California—can in an instant turn cunning and dishonest, seizing whatever means seem necessary, imagining the hoped-for end can remain untainted. I need not speak of the Republican and Democratic parties, mockers of the ordinary citizen's ideals, of America's support of tyranny and corruption, or of the astonishing greed and moral indifference of both public officials and some members of public, whether the payoff be bribery and preferment or those welfare checks drawn by the affluent in Florida on vacation. And sitting in rooms with other artists—sculptors, painters, composers, writers, people whose work I believe to be serious and authentic—I have noticed how frequently, if not infallibly, they react to all these varieties of falsity with stammering, fist-banging rage. In the redness of their faces, the pitch of their voices (not all, of course, shout; some speak quietly, a few make bitter jokes), these artists are not different from the typical Milwaukee banker speaking angrily of the Jews, or the racial fanatic speaking angrily of niggers or honkies; but what these artists care about—what they rave or mourn or bitterly joke about—is the forms of truth: justice, fairness, accuracy.

It is of course far from true that artists are the only honest and compassionate men and women to be found or even that all artists are decent people. But it is true, I think, that the best sort of artist is always, has always been, an enemy of all that is shoddy or false in the world around him and will not hide the fact. The reason, I think, is that the tradition of his art—in the writer's case, the tradition running from Homer, Virgil, Dante, and Shakespeare to the best, most persuasive contemporary novelists and poets—has set before him and filled his heart with an idea of the good which is incomparably more attractive than the filth and foolishness around him, so that when he's wakened from his trance, his artist's dream, he comes up raging like a madman. This is a modern way of saying what Plato meant when he described the artist as "mad." It is not that the artist is possessed by a god—or not in any sense that I'm able to understand. But out of the fullness of the tradition of his art, and out of his deep pleasure in struggling at art himself, he has chosen, irrevocably, art over life. Art possesses him, establishing his norms, which are not the world's norms; hence he is saner than the world, and daemonically mad.

This alienation from the world's normal values (or general lack of them) is often reflected in another, more ordinary alienation, the social displacement which occurs when Dr. Johnson walks to London, Joseph Conrad leaves Poland, Joyce goes to Paris or Faulkner to Hollywood, or the contemporary novelist leaves Harlem, Brooklyn, Texas, Ohio, or Nebraska for Academia. Such displacement is so common in the lives of artists as almost to be a law of artistic success. (For the roaming Celtic bard, in fact, it *was* a law.) It is true that cities are the seats of culture, the homes of patrons, theaters, academies, museums, and galleries, so that the country boy has almost no choice but to head for the city if he wants to be an artist. The situation of the immigrant's son—the young Bernard Malamud, for instance—is parallel, though his move is from one part of the city to another. In the unlucky, social displacement leads to maladjustment and to art that whimpers or snarls. In the lucky, it leads to a healthy doubleness of vision, the healthy alternative—crucial in art—to disorientation and emotional insecurity, the anxiety and ambivalence of the neurotic.

The two most eminently sane poets who have ever written in English, Chaucer and Shakespeare, are both people who moved from one locale and station to another, somewhat more prestigious; and a part of their greatness lies in their having found, through the medium of poetry, ways of reconciling conflicts between the old and the new. To the aristocratic activites of diplomacy and poetry, Chaucer brought an imperfectly renounced middle-class mode of thinking and feeling. Whatever mundane considerations may have contributed to his course of life (ambition, greed, duty), it is evident that when Chaucer looked at aristocratic French and Italian poetry, with its self-consciously elevated diction, its intense intellectuality of form, and its elevated feeling, he looked with great interest but also a skeptical eye. His first long poem, the *Book of the Duchess,* though original in many ways, was at least partly an imitation of the effeminate elegance of such poets as Machaut and Froissart; but even here, and far more noticeably in his mature work, Chaucer plays this elegance against the blunt common sense of his vintry and civil-service background. In the *House of Fame,* in the *Troilus,* and, above all, in the *Canterbury Tales,* he finds ways of asserting what is good in both the aristocratic style of life and the plain style. At those points the two come together, and at those points where their disparity is most pronounced (for instance, in the juxtaposition of the *Knight's Tale* and the *Miller's Tale*), the truth of human experience is, as Dante says, "released."

In the same way, Shakespeare's clowns (Peter Quince in *A Midsummer Night's Dream,* for instance) urgently comment on the world that smiles, mistakenly aloof, at all their antics. Peter Quince is a system of feelings Shakespeare brought with him, perhaps somewhat unwillingly, from Stratford. We need not insist on Freud's word *guilt* in describing such phenomena. We may as readily say *burden,* or *loss.* As often as not, the sense of loss is in the times, not just the poet. Those great periods when old ideas and assumptions are being lost—as in Dante's Florence or Shakespeare's London—are often artistically productive.

The trouble with psychological approaches to creativity is that they tend to oversimplify the nature of the artist's wound. Psychoanalytic theory, as psychoanalysts themselves have often remarked, was developed to deal not with healthy people but with people who have problems—people who cannot stand height or cannot touch doorknobs or cannot stop dreaming the same dream. Artists are singularly complex and as a rule have not one wound to deal with but many, all more or less central to the artist's psyche. We may say that Dante was tortured by sexual guilt or by guilt over Cavalcanti's death (we may be wrong in both cases), but he may well have been equally frustrated by political reversals, by personal betrayals, by loss of property, by his marriage, by exile and physical pain, and by the annoyance which attended his recognition of imperfections in his poetry. Normally, perhaps, the artist is a man who is, as the psychotherapist Jay Haley once remarked, "too complicated to choose a convenient madness." To say that Chaucer had a driving need to resolve a conflict of class loyalties is not to deny that he may have suffered also a conflict of political loyalties— to the absolutist, King Richard, on the one hand, and to the moderate, John of Gaunt, on the other—a conflict, too, of feeling against Christian doctrine, "celestial love" versus an emphatic delight in the bawdy.

But though psychological theory is often all but useless, it can at times provide a focus. For instance, it can help us distinguish between good and bad literature in terms of how the artist's manner of dealing with his troubles compares with the sick man's manner.

The characteristic of all schizophrenic speech—as I mentioned earlier in another connection—is that it denies one or more of the necessary elements of sane communication. If the speaker denies that he is himself, asserting that he's God, speaks gibberish, insists that the hospital is an airbase, or calls his listener Napoleon, he's crazy. How crazy, in these terms, is the writer of poetry or fiction?

Not at all. The writer is fully conscious of what he's

up to when he claims to be not James Joyce but Stephen Dedalus, writes the seeming gibberish of *Finnegans Wake*, pretends to be in Ireland when he's sitting in France, and solemnly, cunningly maintains that the book is for no one. Art imitates insanity and borrows most of the madman's methods (on which more later), but as long as it is art it is only an imitation. The writer's use of a fictitious persona no more qualifies as psychotic than a child's playing fireman or an actor's playing Macbeth. Accidents may happen, but they're irrelevant. When an actor thinks he *is* the character—as happened to Dickens on several occasions when he was performing onstage—he is no longer working as an actor using but controlling his imagination; he has turned madman.

I need not dilate on so obvious a point. Let me hurry on. Some writers do sometimes deny their identity, not from madness but from a more trivial instability, and their art suffers for it; that is, turns creepy. Writers can affect a high style and do it with self-conscious irony, as Auden does in his better poetry, or they can do it without irony because they've forgotten who they are. Auden uses such irony in the last lines of his well-known sonnet, "The Hour-glass Whispers to the Lion's Paw." Let me quote the whole poem.

> The hour-glass whispers to the lion's paw,
> The clocktower tells the gardens day and night
> How many errors Time has patience for,
> How wrong they are in being always right.
> But Time, however loud its chimes, or deep,
> However fast its falling torrent flows,
> Has never put the lion off his leap,
> Or shaken the assurance of a rose.
> For they, it seems, care only for success,
> While we choose words according to their sound
> And judge a problem by its awkwardness;

> And Time, with us, was always popular;
> When have we not preferred some going round
> To going straight to where we are?*

At the risk of belaboring the obvious, let me mention that the word *popular* here is artificially, one might say affectedly, extended, as is much of the poem; but the extension, here and throughout, is in control, part of the poem's subject. (Consciousness of Time makes us poets and mathematicians; lions and roses—and by implication, certain unpleasant sorts of people—are more efficient.) All the cadenced, almost tortuously elegant lines of the poem ("When have we not") collapse into—and make their point by contrast to—the flat speech of the poem's final line. If Auden is posturing, as Pound and Eliot so often did and as Guy Davenport does, he knows it and has, like them, his excellent reasons. On the other hand, as Longinus long ago pointed out, not all writers who pursue elegance know what they're about. Most falsify their true feelings by adopting the mannerisms of some imaginary ideal speaker, someone like John Milton. No example of this is really necessary, but for fun I offer the last lines (the first would do as well) of Lucretia Maria Davidson's—alas, now forgotten—poem to the family clock:

> Friend of my youth! ere from its mouldering clay
> My joyful spirit wings to heaven its way,
> Oh, may'st thou watch beside my aching head,
> And tell how fast Time flits with feathered tread.

The lines are a delight to analyze (the simultaneously mouldering clay and the aching head, the ingenious feather trick), but I forbear.

A writer need not fake elegance to belie himself. He can as much deny his nature by insistent obscenity—a

*From W. H. Auden, *Collected Poems,* edited by Edward Mendelson. Copyright 1940 and renewed 1968 by W. H. Auden. Reprinted by permission of Random House, Inc.

brainless pursuit of the modern extreme of what once was called the "low style"—or by an insistent eschewing of sentiment—as in Hemingway and many a later writer—which invariably ends up screamingly sentimental. Or he may go for the good, old-fashioned sentimental, saying sappy things, untrue things, not bothering with proofs because he believes all sensible people must agree with him. In this vein James Wright is occasionally an offender, as in these lines:

> I was only a boy.
>
> I swam all the way through a tear on a dead face.
>
> America is dead
> And it is the only country I had.
>
> Harry. Harry.
> Are you still alive? [20]

This refusal of writers to admit or bother to discover who they are—the sacrifice of thought for pious rant—is one of the most noticeable and tiresome faults of contemporary literature, though hardly a fault invented in our time. The Romantic age produced more Southeys than Keatses, as the American version produced more Lucretia Maria Davidsons than Poes. It has always been easier to define one's character in terms of those things one is not than to say what one is, and easier still if the things one is not are all straw men, like the Zeboamites invented by the Mormons. This is the "new sentimentality," as A. M. Tibbetts calls it:

The new sentimentality in fiction is characterized mainly by the emotionalism of intellectualized self-pity, dislike, or even of hatred. The new sentimentalist customarily disapproves of his world. The more civilized and decent it is, the more he disapproves of it. He finds refuge in the pedantic play of his mind over the flaws in the world and in himself; for ultimately he secretly dislikes himself (the unhappy Outsider) as much as he loathes the bulk of men who live on the Inside. He considers Insiders beneath his contempt, yet he writes long books oozing with contempt for them—that unthinking crowd of human beings who are stupid enough to ignore him and sometimes even to be happy.[21]

The healthy alternative to the false voice, of course, is the true one; and remembering how silly a false voice sounds, we remind ourselves of the aesthetic—to say nothing of the human—value of the true. That is what makes younger poets like Carl Dennis stand out. These lines, for instance, from a poem about an art museum:

> So he looks hard at the painted scene.
> Maybe the boy with the bird and the whale
> Would tell him something useful about the soul
> If only he hadn't neglected his studies.
> He needs a teacher, he thinks, to help him see,
> And looking around the room discovers me
> Looking at him with my sympathetic stare.
> If he comes this way I hope to tell him the truth
> About the shortage of teachers everywhere.[22]

It's the same power, that magical truth of voice, that we're first caught up by in the best poems of Linda Pastan, Dave Smith, Galway Kinell, Donald Finkel, or among older poets Mona Van Duyn, Howard Nemerov, Anthony Hecht, and William Meredith. Not that such perfect, clear health in art proves health in life—as no one knew better than the late Anne Sexton. Even in her darkest poems, the voice is sure, the expression of even the most terrible feelings accurate. But her best, I think, is in the poems in which she fights with all her heart against the illness which eventually killed her—poems electric with a voltage beyond madness, the energy of ferocious struggle against madness, an almost frightening determination to affirm life and love—such poems as the painfully triumphant "Live," at the end of the volume *Live or Die*, or in the same volume, "For the Year of the Insane: A Prayer," which closes,

O Mary, open your eyelids.
I am in the domain of silence,
the kingdom of the crazy and the sleeper.
There is blood here
and I have eaten it.
O mother of the womb,
did I come for blood alone?
O little mother,
I am in my own mind.
I am locked in the wrong house.[23]

What happened in the best poetry of Anne Sexton is that art's gift for playing roles gave her distance, helped her see and survive, helped her escape from the mad-woman into the artist. Even a thoroughly sane poet needs the distance of the poetic dream to get life into focus, for the terrible truth, Anne Sexton knew, is that life does not care about any of us: by our existence we may celebrate and intensify the moment, but we're as expendable as frogs. So Linda Pastan writes, speaking in the voice of Penelope,

Meanwhile the old wars
go on, their dim music
can be heard even at night.
You leave each morning,
soon our son will follow.
Only my weaving is real.[24]

Another way one may turn his speech psychotic, ac-cording to the formula with which we started out, is by speaking gibberish. It goes almost without saying that gibberish—or something that at first glance looks like gibberish—is one of the most interesting things an art-ist can create. That statement will not seem curious to the experienced reader, but it is interesting and a little surprising to notice that hacks and primitive artistic dabblers—always so quick to steal true art's devices—almost never use gibberish. It veers too close to true poetry, to the absolute seriousness of the divinely mad. For true poetry it has always been one of the noblest inventions, now riddling, now oracular, now heightening a dramatic effect in Dostoevski, Dickens, or Melville. Shakespeare made it his specialty, not only in the ravings and ramblings of characters like Lear and Hamlet, the pointed lunacy of fools and bumpkins, but also in more out-of-the-way places, like the syntactically blurry underwater song "Full Fathom Five." In modern fiction seeming gibberish provides some of the most moving and thought-provoking passages in the work of Joyce, Dos Passos, Anderson, Faulkner, Ralph Ellison, William Burroughs, John Hawkes, William Gaddis, and Joyce Carol Oates—to name only the most obvious.

Clearly there is nothing psychotic in all this. Even in Burroughs' *The Ticket That Exploded*, where throughout the closing section we read nonsense phrases produced by a looped and scrambled tape of the novel's earlier sections, the babble is not in fact senseless. The threat against humanity in every Burroughs novel is that we may allow ourselves to be destroyed by our own accidental nature if we make no choices among accidents, such as the rise of mechanization, seen at its worst in behaviorist mind-altering and in mechanized politics, both of which are amoral and tyrannical. We are ourselves the ticket that exploded (DNA-determined creatures in overpopulation) and almost all that we see and feel is accident folding over accident; yet we do see and feel and can make choices: the novel is the proof. Not at first understanding what they are, thinking them stream-of-consciousness sections like those earlier in the novel, we read the garbled sections in *Ticket* exactly as we read the intentional gibberish of *Finnegans Wake*, and here as there we see things, make discoveries, find good. What is best in life, the willingness of consciousness to respond and judge, is strengthened by the right kind of gibberish—a serious and decent novel fractured to all possible symbol and phrase combinations. As for what is ugly in life, Burroughs (or rather Brion Gysin, author of the novel's "closing message") speaks of people's mindless and machinelike repetition of old opinions, prejudices—"shop keeper snarling cops pale nigger killing eyes reflecting society's disapproval fucking queers i say shoot them"—as a vast tape recording, and advises:

only way to break the inexorable down spiral of ugly uglier ugliest recording and playback is with counter-recording and playback the first step is to isolate and cut association lines of the control machine   carry a tape recorder with you and record all the ugliest stupidest things cut your ugly tapes in together speed up slow down play backwards inch the tape   you will hear one ugly voice and see one ugly spirit is made of ugly old prerecordings   the more you run the tapes through and cut them up the less power they will have cut the prerecordings into air into thin air. [25]

What must be remembered is that in good poetry and fiction the writer speaks, first, to clarify in his own mind what he thinks and feels and, second, to make that clear to somebody else, on the assumption that the reader has sometimes felt, or can now be encouraged to feel, the same. Molly Bloom's soliloquy in *Ulysses* is as it is becaue it cannot be otherwise and mean what it has to mean. The same is true of *The Sound and the Fury*, though not of all the queer writing in Faulkner. When Faulkner's mixed-up language and structure go awry, they do so because the writer has fallen from a basic concern with matter to a self-conscious concern with manner: not sure what he's trying to get hold of, Faulkner at times tries to whip up his inspiration by incantation, forgetting that once the incantation was designed to call up subject matter known to be there: the dizzy breathlessness of the librarian, for instance, who rushes with her news, in the prologue to the first edition of *The Sound and the Fury*, to Jason's store.

Every person who wants desperately to write, or desperately enough at least to go through the enormous inconvenience even bad writing imposes on one's life, and who, when he or she sits down to it, focuses all attention on finding *for its own sake* some new mode, some new bafflement for the defenseless reader, has misunderstood what makes one sit down at the typewriter in the first place. He justifies his existence by showing the world, as if it cared, that he is a Writer. But the stylemaker knows, even if his critics miss it, that the whole thing is a delusion. He has not answered the voice of the wound—"You're nothing, not even a writer"—he has merely drowned it out for a moment and unwittingly fed it ammunition—"You're worse than nothing, a fraud." On the other hand, of course, the writer who does nothing to achieve a necessary and necessarily personal style, but speaks the banalities and rhythms of others, is in no better shape and stands in even greater danger of tumbling into nonsense.

Sane speech also admits its context. The schizophrenic, to be cured, must be persuaded to face the fact that he is standing in his mother's house or the hospital or wherever he is. The writer who creates, who does not merely spin his wheels producing nothing, understands where he is, where his world is. He does not simplify or evade.

Obviously the writer who knows about his time and place need not therefore limit himself to realism. Writers of fantasy, science fiction, or retold-myths like Gide's *Theseus* have often given expression to the deepest concerns of their time. J. R. R. Tolkien in his Ring trilogy sums up more powerfully than any realist could do the darkness of total war and the essential opposition of evil and good in the shadow of some monstrously destructive power. (Though the atomic bomb was not yet invented when Tolkien wrote, its general principle had been understood for years in England and was the common whisper in educated circles.) The Ring trilogy presents, among other things, Tolkien's understanding of the threat of English annihilation and his intuition of still more terrible things to come. Fantasy writing, of course, nearly always comments on the time and place that produced it, from *The Arabian Nights* to *Gulliver's Travels* to the best of contemporary fantasy.

Social context is of course more directly important for those writers whose primary concern is with the evils of society, political systems, and the like. Context is at the heart of the matter for Negro, Jewish, and regional novelists and poets, for city writers whose chief complaint is alienation or the mechanization of modern life, and for novelists and poets interested in, say, "Americanism." In this crowd most recent and contemporary novelists and poets fit, and one sign of how bad most contemporary literature is, is the extent to which writers simplify and melodramatize for lack of real understanding of the social groups or general forces now at work. We have seen in recent years a few great novelists and poets like Pär Lagerkvist, who have interested themselves not only in the anguish of the social moment but also in a larger or at least more enduring problem: metaphysical anguish. For them the question is not merely right assessment of the motivation and character of individuals and groups around them but also the deeper matter of understanding contemporary science and philosophy and the climate of feeling these express. But clearly such writers are exceedingly rare in comparison with writers like Robert Coover in *The Public Burning*, who reduces large and complex forces to humorless comic-strip cartoons, or Thomas Pynchon, who, in *Gravity's Rainbow*, carelessly praises the schlock of the past (King Kong, etc.) and howls against the schlock of the present which, he thinks, is numbing and eventually will kill us. We may defend *Gravity's Rainbow* as a satire, but whether it is meant to be satire or sober analysis is not clear. It is a fact that, even to the rainbow of bombs said to be circling us, the world is not as Pynchon says it is. That may not matter in this book—the reader must judge—but it would be disastrous in a book impossible to read as satire.

Finally, sane speech is speech to someone. The creative process is vitiated if the writer writes only for himself. This is not to say that all good writing is "popular." In the modern world, with its thousands of colleges and universities, it is absurd to imagine that any writer exists who is of such genius that no man of his time can enjoy and understand him. The wail of modern poets and novelists—that art has lost its audience—is a piece of what Hobbes called insignificant speech. The audience of Joyce, Pound, Beckett, even Burroughs, is enormous. The writer who is out to do something, not merely pass the time, must recognize that nothing prevents his trying to talk to readers as sensitive and intelligent as himself. True, commercial editors may not gamble on his work. But to write badly because otherwise one might not get published is useless compromise.

On the other hand, if an intelligent and sensitive writer would rather communicate with the general public, let him learn the conventions of popular fiction and turn them to his purpose. As John le Carré, Isaac Asimov, Peter Beagle, Curtis Harnak, and many others have shown, one need not be a fool or a compromiser to write a mystery story, a sci-fi or fantasy, or a book about growing up in Iowa. The fool is the man who arrogantly denies the worth and common sense of the people to whom he pretends to speak. In short, another test of creative energy is the test of efficient communication: to what extent does the artist know whom he is dealing with, telling him what he needs to know, not less.

A great deal more might be said on this subject, but not by me.

I have spoken of art and psychotic non-communication; one might also compare art and ordinary neurosis. It would serve no purpose to do so here at length, but to illustrate what I mean let me mention just two of the more common neurotic symptoms, displaced emotion—love or hate directed not at the thing actually loved or hated but at something toward which the neurotic feels indifferent, or would if he were well—and symptomatic repetition, the common "tic."

Artists, even good ones, sometimes do displace emotion. When it happens, the result is either sentimentality (sometimes in the form of nastiness) or hollowness. As everyone knows, in Eugene Field's once popular bit of doggerel, "Little Boy Blue," the emotion directed toward "the little toy dog . . . all covered with dust" (but sturdy and staunch he stands) and "the little toy soldier . . . red with rust" (and his musket moulds in his hands) parallels neurotic displacement. What Field's narrator really experiences is self-pity at the loss of his child, some years ago, and pride in his own faithfulness (not that of the toys). Except for these emotions he would not have left the child's bedroom untouched, as a kind of shrine. The reader senses the distortion and draws back in embarrassment. With the same feeling of distaste one shrinks from Pound's self-righteous mistranslation of "The Seafarer." Of the better known writers now at work, nearly all are at least oc-

PRINCIPLES OF ART AND CRITICISM

casionally guilty of emotional displacement. One is
tempted to believe that bigotry is in, fair-mindedness
and even humorous detachment out. The exceptions, of
course, are a pleasure to encounter—writers like John
Irving, whose humor never snipes with mere cruelty,
or poets like Samuel Hazo, James B. Hall, Robert Pack,
Ruth Fainlight (in her later poems), or, as I said before,
Linda Paston or Carl Dennis, poets whose expressions
of feeling, whether trivial or deep, ring true.

Hollowness in poetry or fiction shows itself mainly in
the writer's exaggerated interest in the trimmings of his
drama—in compulsively elaborate description which
does not feel to the reader like description of objects
loved or hated but seems creative emotion (concentra-
tion) arbitrarily directed. So one reacts to the imagistic
excesses of Kazantzakis' *The Odyssey: A Modern Sequel*
or to the pseudo-Arabic lushness of Durrell's Alex-
andria quartet. Hollowness may also show itself in
compulsive tinkering with trivial but omnipresent
symbolism. This is of course not to say that symbolism
is a bad thing and should be banished; it is merely to
say that to work at all, symbolism must work forcefully,
partly below consciousness, generated by and com-
menting on the dramatic conflict.

As for neurotic repetition, its most obvious evidence
is the writer's treatment of the same central question
and situation in work after work, with no sign of
growth. D. H. Lawrence is an example, as Daniel Weiss
pointed out some years ago in *Oedipus at Nottingham*.
Healthy fiction is dialectic: the writer's understanding
increases with each book he solves. Consider the progression of thought in Yeats, or in Wallace Stevens, or
notice the growth of Faulkner's understanding of the
Snopes family from their first introduction down to *The
Mansion*.

Another form of neurotic repetition is the fossilized

198

emotion regularly triggered by certain ideas (rote religion, polite manners, and so forth) in the late works of Tolstoy. What fossilized emotion naturally suggests is that the wound has not been healed but merely calmed by morphine, or compensated by a tic. The same sort of fossilized emotion is visible, of course, in any writer's witting or unwitting repetition, throughout a book or canon of books, of some seemingly insignificant word or phrase or detail of description, Faulkner's "myriad" and "apotheosis." A psychoanalyst might be able to figure out, in time, exactly what the nervously repeated word means to the writer, but his findings would be of no interest except, possibly, to the writer and his family. What counts for the reader is that, like a self-regarding, preening style, nervous twitches distract him from the writing to the writer. We suspect that the writer is trying to recapture some earlier, more authentic emotion by repeating himself. Much the same can be said of hysterical style—again D. H. Lawrence is the prime example among major writers, Baraka among minor—that is, a style that screams, endlessly repeating a few ideas or even phrases.

It shouldn't be necessary to compare in more detail than this the ways of art and the ways of neurosis, for the general point is simple: art treats emotion, and when it distorts emotion, it fails in one or another of the ways the neurotic personality fails. Whatever Milton really meant, it is in this sense that we should understand his notion that to write a true poem one must first become a true poet.

Before I leave these musings on art and insanity, I would like to mention and briefly develop certain aspects of one last approach to the whole business, the approach through philosophical speculation. It goes without saying that, exactly as with art, nothing an old-style philosopher says can be proved except by the tests of inclusiveness and internal consistency; but philosophical speculation can nevertheless be fascinating and, insofar as one believes it, instructive.[26] R. G. Collingwood develops, in *The New Leviathan*, a theory of the rise of consciousness through the conflicts of instinctual passions, and in his *Principles of Art* he shows, somewhat confusedly (he wrote in haste, trying to outrace a sickness entailing brain deterioration), the implications of his general theory for art. Suddenly made aware of a dangerous bull in a field, Collingwood says, a man responds with two simultaneous and contradictory animal emotions, fear and anger, each of which urges a different course of action: to run or to fight. If the emotional reactions, or "charges," are of equal strength, the man either stands frozen or else rises to consciousness and chooses between the emotions. If he can do the latter it is because he recognizes the emotions; in other words, has risen to what William James called the first stage of consciousness—"Ha! There goes the same thing I saw before again!" This rise into consciousness is in effect man's first creative act—one requiring an enormous amount of mental power—and, according to Collingwood, it is also man's first act of freedom. Consciousness means consciousness of self; it resides in naming one's mental processes, reasoning about the names, and then naming each successive deduction or connection.

The creative thinking involved in art is an extraordinarily complicated version of this same activity of mind. The urgings of passion, both present and remembered, provide the poet with his "fantasy"—the raw material of his fable. The necessity of choosing between conflicting emotions or emotionally charged ideas, the necessity of choosing what to put first, and the necessity of meeting the arbitrary demands of form (for example, rhyme) fully awaken the artist's critical consciousness, both intellectual and organic testing processes, and govern what it is that he puts down. In revising, the creative artist repeats this process, coming with each revision to fuller and more totally conscious awareness of his feelings. Throughout this discussion, I should make plain, *feeling* means idea as well as raw emotion. The name of the feeling—in other words, the idea of its whatness, the feeling articulated—retains at least some of the emotion's charge.

If this seems strange, consider the fact that a man trained in autohypnosis can glance at the corner of the room, say seven numbers, and drop instantly into total recall of a particular past experience. The hypnotic key (the group of numbers) is the *name* of an amazingly complex body of feelings, memories, and so forth. In a light trance state these may be "recollected in tranquillity" in the sense that the subject can detach himself from the recollection and know that, say, the train he remembers bearing down on him did not at that time kill him. In a deep trance such detachment is less likely.

The phenomenon of the hypnotic key provides a clue to something not mentioned in Collingwood's description of creative process. Autohypnosis of a certain kind is at the core of artistic creativity. Whereas the usual autohypnotist is a man who has trained himself to recall any given situation or feeling state by means of a key, the good creative artist is a man who has learned, normally without so obvious a key (it may be the apple core in the poet's desk drawer), to drop at will almost anywhere he wishes in his experience, recapturing an infinite variety of impressions from the past—though he may not have a clear idea of where in his past they come from. Only the greatest writers, among them Joyce, Tolstoy, and Proust, show this talent developed to the maximum. It may be, as Freud and others have thought, that the artist is someone who never lost the eidetic memory normal in childhood. Certainly the parallel though rather different descriptions by Coleridge and Wordsworth of waning imagination might be viewed as chronicles of waning eidetic recall. In any event, it seems certain that a writer is someone who has developed to a high degree an ability to remember things and to alter them at will, for instance placing imagined characters in remembered situations, placing remembered characters in imagined situations, and so forth; and it seems to me in these imaginative moments the writer is certainly in some sort of trance.

At certain times in my own experience the sense of entrancement has been vivid. Several years ago when my wife was in the hospital and I was under emotional strain I worked on a piece of fiction almost steadily for three days and nights, stopping only for brief hospital visits, coffee, and cigarettes. When I finished, exhausted, I went to sit on the couch in the living room of our apartment, drinking a last cup of coffee before going to bed. As I sat, passive, it came to me that the room was full of a mumble of voices much like the mumble one hears as one slips into dreams, except much louder, as loud as the voices at an ordinary, crowded party; and the room was full, too, of obscure shapes, forms as large and solid as bears or people but unstable: by the slightest effort I could change them into anything or anyone I pleased. All this surprised me but did not at all stir fear or anxiety, because what was happening seemed clear—in fact, I seemed to recognize the experience. While I was writing, earlier, I had been daydreaming similar creatures and voices: a light touch of intellect made the creatures into people who showed me how an imaginary line of action must go if it was to be true to the real process of life. Now, as the controlling intellect relaxed, the darker machinery was running overtime, without purpose, filling my room with things not really there. Metaphor and fact had become one.

That, I think, is about as mad as art gets. The writer and the psychotic make use of the same faculty and similar energy, the same ability to escape external time and space. If it is true that the motive force of this energy is some tension in the life of the artist or madman—an "ego-wound," the psychologist would say, but Collingwood allows us to extend this to mean any driving need for understanding or choosing between the rival claims of intense brute or human feelings—then a proper use of artistic energy is one which treats the tension, makes decisions about it rather than evading it. The artist is free, the psychotic—helplessly driven by his fear—is not. The theoretical border between art and madness seems to be, then, that the artist can wake up and the psychotic cannot. In fact, though, the difference must be one of degree. Psychotics, we know, can snap out of it, and sometimes do, and an occasional artist relinquishes his hold. Shakespeare understood this. When Hamlet plays mad, he takes a step toward real madness. Sanity is remembering the purpose of the game.

We began with the observation that what distinguishes great art is its sanity. Now we must admit that the observation is a half-truth. Art's essential method verges on the psychotic: the artist creates, by the energy of his mind (including his anguish or, at least, concern), prodded and assisted by the substance and conventions of his artistic medium, a world that isn't there, a dream. Other things being equal, the more intensely the artist imagines his dream world, the more fully he surrenders to it, the more passionate his devotion to capturing it in words, images, or music—or, to put it another way, the deeper his trance and the greater his divorce from ordinary reality—the greater is likely to be the effect of the artist's work on the reader, viewer, or listener. So long as the artist avoids what I have described as "hollowness"—that obsessive fussing with the trappings of the vision (decorations of the set, language for the sake of language) which substitutes for true intensity—and so long as the artist is a master of technique, so that no stroke is wasted, no idea or emotion blurred, it is the extravagance of the artist's purposeful self-abandonment to his dream that will determine the dream's power. The true artist plays mad with all his soul, labors at the very lip of the volcano, but remembers and clings to his purpose, which is as strong as the dream. He is not someone possessed, like Cassandra, but a passionate, easily tempted explorer who fully intends to get home again, like Odysseus.

True art is not rabid, though to ordinary mortals some artists may seem just that—to Mrs. Hawthorne, for instance, when Melville came around, crazy-eyed, drunk, and wearing one of those hats, asking to see Nathaniel, who was none too comfortable himself in Melville's presence. The true artist is likely to be furious in the company of cheapness or compromise. (It is careless criticism, not Melville, that forgives Captain Vere.) He may be indifferent to his own welfare, like an Old Testament prophet in the presence of an unjust king. But it is precisely at the point of rabidity that the gifted but false artist—even one as gifted as Ezra Pound—and the true artist part company. True art's divine madness is shot through with love: love of the good, a love proved not by some airy and abstract high-mindedness but by active celebration of whatever good or trace of good can be found by a quick and compassionate eye in this always corrupt and corruptible but god-freighted world. To return one last time to the image of Thor's hammer with which I launched all this, it strikes outward at the trolls, or inward when the trolls have made incursions, not blindly in all directions. It smashes to construct. Most artists will no doubt claim they do just that, and most critics will no doubt claim that they praise only artists who, in one way or another, fight for the good. Some artists and critics tell the truth; some lie. The business of civilization is to pay attention, remembering what is central, remembering that we live or die by the artist's vision, sane or cracked.

NOTES

1. *What Is Art? and Essays On Art*, trans. by Aylmer Maude, The World's Classics edition (London: Oxford University Press, 1969), pp. 286–88.

2. Bruno Bettelheim, *The Uses of Enchantment: The Meaning and Importance of Fairy Tales* (New York: Alfred A. Knopf, Inc., 1976). Some of Bettelheim's explanations of how fairy tales work seem doubtful, to say the least, but there can be no doubt that his main point is convincing, if not downright obvious; that fairy tales educate and liberate children's emotions.

3. Besides "What Is Art?" see especially "On Truth in Art," a comment on folktales, Tolstoy's introductions to S. T. Semenov's Peasant Stories and to the Works of Guy de Maupassant, and the essay "On Art," all included in *What Is Art? and Essays On Art.*

4. Homer's system is examined in detail in *Homer's "Iliad": The Shield of Memory*, by Kenneth Atchity, (Carbondale, Illinois: Southern Illinois University Press, 1977).

5. There are some, these days, who deny that Beatrice was ever anything but a poetic metaphor. Dante did have, after all, twelve children by another woman. Though I am fully persuaded that Beatrice did exist and that Dante loved her, the point is unimportant; in all his writings about his life, Dante treats himself, too, as a poetic metaphor.

6. The thirtieth canto of the *Purgatorio* and the closing cantos of the *Paradiso* might be described as exceptions, but though the tenor at these points may be mystical images of, respectively, the Host and the Trinity, the vehicle is in both cases Beatrice, and the effect seems consciously sexual as well as religious, as it never was in mystical writing. In the first case, in fact, Dante has just finished alluding to Dido's sexual passion for Aeneas, comparing it with his own for his lady.

7. Edgar Allan Poe, *Marginalia*, excerpted in *Edgar Allan Poe—Representative Selections*, ed., Margaret Alterton and Hardin Craig for the American Writers Series (New York: The American Book Company, 1935), p. 412.

8. George Steiner, *The Death of Tragedy* (New York: Alfred A. Knopf, Inc., 1961), p. 127. Much of my argument, here and elsewhere in this book, draws on Steiner.

9. Jean-Paul Sartre, *Being and Nothingness*, trans. by Hazel E. Barnes (New York: Philosophical Library, 1956), pp. 55–56.

10. This is meant as no insult to Chaucer, of course. As I pointed out in *The Poetry of Chaucer* (Carbondale, Illinois: Southern Illinois University Press, 1977), Chaucer was well-acquainted with nominalist theory. His *Canterbury Tales*, as well as some earlier poems, is in part anti-nominalist satire.

11. E. L. Doctorow, *Ragtime* (New York: Random House, 1974), p. 54.

12. *What Is Art?*, p. 21.

13. I. A. Richards, *Principles of Literary Criticism* (New York: Harcourt Brace, 1924), pp. 5–6.

14. Northrop Frye, *The Well-Tempered Critic* (Gloucester, Mass.: Peter Smith, 1963), p. 141.

15. Frye, *The Well-Tempered Critic*, p. 140.

16. Frye, *The Well-Tempered Critic*, p. 141.

17. For the full defense I do not take time for, see Brand Blanshard, *Reason and Goodness* (Atlantic Highlands, N.J.: Humanities Press, 1961).

18. Richards, *Principles of Literary Criticism*, p. 283.

19. Edgar Allan Poe, *The Complete Works* (New York: G. D. Sproul, 1902), ed., J. A. Harrison, vol. 14, pp. 197–98.

20. James Wright, "Heraclitus," in *The Paris Review*, vol. 16, no. 62, pp. 68–69. Reprinted with permission.

21. I copied this comment of Tibbetts' down into a notebook five or six years ago, God knows from where.

22. From Carl Dennis, "Students," in *A House of My Own* (New York: George Braziller, 1974), p. 5. Reprinted with permission of the publisher.

23. From Anne Sexton, "For the Year of the Insane: A Prayer," in *Live or Die* (Boston: Houghton Mifflin, 1966), p. 46. Copyright © 1966 by Anne Sexton. Reprinted with permission.

24. From Linda Pastan, "You Are Odysseus," in *Aspects of Eve* (New York: Liveright, 1975), p. 21. Reprinted with permission.

25. Brion Gysin, "Closing Message," in *The Ticket That Exploded*, second version (New York: Grove Press, 1967), p. 217.

26. In the last few years numerous philosophical speculations on art have appeared, some interesting but almost totally unreadable, like Roman Ingarden's *The Literary Work of Art* (Evanston, Illinois: Northwestern University Press, 1973) and Justus Buchler's *The Main of Light: On the Concept of Poetry* (London: Oxford University Press, 1974), others more approachable, for instance, Mikel Dufrenne's *The Phenomenology of Aesthetic Experience* (Evanston, Illinois: Northwestern University Press, 1973).

INDEX

209

211

SE 27 '82
NO 15 '82
FEB 3
OCT 6
OCT 30 1998
11/6/00

GAYLORD

PRINTED IN U.S.A.

DISCARD

801 G174o
Gardner, John,
On moral fiction / John Gardne

AAC-2059
030101 000

0 0003 0033932 2

Castleton State College